Praise for the Red Ca

MURDER ON A L

MW00453857

"Delicious! A great read written by someone who knows the behind the scenes world of filmmaking...A winner!"

– Kathryn Leigh Scott,
Author of the Jinx Fogarty Mysteries

"Loved this book! The characters are well-drawn and it's cleverly plotted. Totally engrossing...I felt as though I was actually on a movie set. The author is well-versed in her setting and she is able to keep the reader in suspense. I can't wait for the second book in the series."

– Marianna Heusler,
Edgar-Nominated Author

MURDER ON THE HALF SHELL (#2)

"This nicely woven drama once again gave us an insight into catering (what a hard job) while keeping me intrigued in a mystery with some twisty currents that was hard to put down. With a nice island flavor, a nice puzzling mystery and a great cast of characters, this was a very enjoyable read."

– *Dru's Book Musings*

"The writing is fun, quirky and engaging. The character development between the lead character and her love interest is well done and believable. This book has several of my favorite things at the forefront: movies, murder, and food prep."

– *Goodreads*

MURDER
ON A
SILVER PLATTER

The Red Carpet Catering Mystery Series
by Shawn Reilly Simmons

MURDER ON A SILVER PLATTER (#1)
MURDER ON THE HALF SHELL (#2)
MURDER ON A DESIGNER DIET (#3)
(June 2016)

MURDER
ON A
SILVER PLATTER

A RED CARPET CATERING MYSTERY

SHAWN REILLY
SIMMONS

HENERY PRESS

MURDER ON A SILVER PLATTER
A Red Carpet Catering Mystery
Part of the Henery Press Mystery Collection

Second Edition
Trade paperback edition | February 2016

Henery Press, LLC
www.henerypress.com

ISBN-13: 978-1-943390-57-1

Printed in the United States of America

To Matthew and Russell,
who make everything possible.

ACKNOWLEDGMENTS

Thanks from the bottom of my heart to everyone who helped make this dream a reality. They say it takes a village to raise a child, and I've found the same thing applies to writing a book.

None of this would have been possible without my mom, Stephanie Reilly, who encouraged me from the start to pursue my dreams, wherever they may take me. She's a "Go Big or Go Home" kind of mom, and that encouragement has pushed me through the years to reach for and fully pursue my goals and passions. Mom's love of books, especially crime fiction and mysteries, was passed on to me at a very young age, and for that I'm forever grateful.

Huge thanks goes out to my sister, Erin Reilly Hawkins, for bringing me along as her assistant chef to all of those dinner parties, and for getting me hired onto the theatrical catering crew. We've had a lot of fun in the kitchen, even when the food started flying.

I would not be the person I am today without Malice Domestic, and I'd like to thank the entire Board, past and present, for their constant support and encouragement. I must give special thanks to Verena Rose, Harriette Sacker, Marian Lesko, Angel Trapp, Anne Murphy and Tonya Spratt-Williams for their love, for being my family, there whenever I need you.

I could not even begin to list all of the mystery authors who have encouraged me to pursue this dream. I am so grateful to be part of this hugely supportive community of writers. You all know who you are, and you have my heartfelt thanks.

I am fortunate to be surrounded by a smart and quirky group of gals, who I've come to rely on for support, a laugh or some good advice, pretty much daily. Thanks to Krista L, Julia B, Kelly L, Stephanie B, Kimberly G, Melanie B, and Martha B, for all the happy hours, funny texts, bottles of wine, dirty jokes, book recommendations and random movie quotes that keep me going on a daily basis.

Thanks to Ildy Shannon for being my first reader, and for all of your sage advice. Thanks to Colleen Shannon for being my biggest cheerleader, and for doing most of my worrying for me.

My undying gratitude and thanks go to Kendel Lynn, Art Molinares and everyone else at Henery Press for taking a chance on me and Penelope. I'm so thrilled to be a part of your ever-growing empire. The support and guidance from Rachel Jackson and Erin George, editors extraordinaire, leaves me speechless. I've never worked with a more positive, upbeat group of people and I'm grateful beyond words.

This book would not have happened without Matthew and Russell, who are convinced I can do anything, even when I'm not so sure. Their love and support is everything—they are my heart.

This book is about family, the one you're born with and the one you create as you go. I'd like to thank everyone in mine, near and far, here and gone, with all my heart.

CHAPTER 1

He'd done it again. Torn off into the freezing night without a care in the world, disregarding the feelings of everyone he'd left behind, oblivious to how they would worry about him being alone out in the cold.

"Damn dog," Arlena muttered, clouds of steam puffing from her lips.

Penelope nodded stiffly, her body rigid against the cold. "You can say that again."

Their boots crunched through the sparkling white snow as they made their way down the road, ponytails swinging. One of them shouted "Zazoo!" every few steps.

Zazoo had scampered off right after the electricity went out, the outage conveniently disabling the electric doggie door in the kitchen and the invisible fence that surrounded their property. Zazoo had slipped out and his sapphire studded white leather collar didn't zap his neck as he passed over the barrier he had memorized at the edge of the lawn. After that he ran as hard and as fast as he could, his tiny little legs kicking against his belly as he scampered down the road, led only by the scents of the night and various calling cards from his canine neighbors.

"Zazoo! I can't believe he did this to me again," Arlena said. She darted her flashlight beam around as they walked. "Thanks for looking for him with me."

Penelope held her hands together in front of her mouth, wishing for warmth and breathing hot air through her mittens. "Not a problem," she said, even though it kind of was. Maybe more of an inconvenience. It was definitely the worst night and time to be out on the road. The power had been out for several hours and the snow plows had only been down the streets once or twice to push aside more than eight inches of heavy snow. Penelope had no idea how they were going to find the little Bich-Poo. Zazoo was fluffy and white, blending in with the snow, and without any functioning street lamps to guide the way, it was almost impossible to see anything. Penelope thought it was unlikely they'd find the little five-pound dog out here in the dark. It would be a miracle if they ended up finding him before he froze to death.

They heard a plow somewhere far off and both glanced towards the sound. The sidewalks hadn't been shoveled yet, so the two of them trudged down the middle of the road. A row of magnificent houses closed tight against the cold sat on their right, tall iron gates guarding their long driveways. The back end of Glendale's country club and golf course sat on their left, now just a wide open field covered in white. The moonless sky offered no help and it was difficult to see much around them. Penelope didn't want to say so out loud, but she hadn't noticed any footprints or signs of anything living.

"I can't believe he would run off like this again. I do everything for him and he takes off the first chance he gets." Arlena's big brown eyes began tearing up. Penelope couldn't tell whether her friend's tears were from Zazoo's acts of betrayal or the bitterly cold air. She didn't think Arlena's dog was smart enough to actively plan elaborate escapes. He was an opportunist at best.

"He always comes home eventually," Penelope offered, rubbing her friend's arm. Arlena's stylishly sleek ski jacket made a whooshing sound under her mitten. Arlena Madison always looked polished and put together, even in a lost dog crisis on a deserted New Jersey road. Tight black leggings hugged her calves and her feet were warmed by fur lined Michael Kors snow boots, which perfectly highlighted her long toned legs. She topped off her dog searching outfit with an on-trend knit deerstalker hat in soft pink with matching scarf and gloves. Her long black hair hung in a shiny silk ponytail and her makeup was perfection, expertly applied.

Penelope had thrown on a puffy coat also, but hers was faded red, a few seasons old and didn't fit quite right. It was actually one of Arlena's castoffs from an apparent grunge phase. She had the clothes on from when she had been comfortable in the den before they headed out: yoga pants, a slouchy sweater and big fuzzy socks. She'd been curled up in front of the fireplace in her cozy chair, a glass of wine in her hand and an Agatha Christie novel in her lap. Then the power had blown and she'd been recruited to leave the house on a dog hunt. As they headed out to look for Zazoo she'd stuffed her thickly socked feet into her well-worn, salty black snow boots and pulled a simple blue knit cap over her straight blond hair, which she'd tied in a messy ponytail at the base of her neck, never once thinking about coordinating her outfit. Penelope looked like she was heading out for a deep sea fishing excursion while Arlena could be heading to the hottest club in the city.

"Why don't I head back towards the house and you keep going? Maybe if we split up we'll find him faster," Arlena said, her words chattering out through her perfect white teeth and painted pink lips. Penelope was momentarily distracted when she noticed that Arlena's lipstick perfectly matched her hat and scarf. She absentmindedly swiped a cherry lip balm wand she found in her coat pocket across her lips.

"That's a good idea. Maybe he's already home. Watch out

for cars on the road. They might not see you," Penelope warned.

"Do you want the flashlight?" Arlena asked.

"That's okay. I have a flashlight app. I'll be fine," Penelope said, waving her phone halfheartedly at Arlena.

"Thanks again, Pen," Arlena said before they headed off in opposite directions.

"Call me if you find him," Penelope said over her shoulder after she'd walked a few feet. She could feel the cold coming in through her yoga pants and wished she had taken the time to put on some long johns. Feeling her knees start to numb, she pressed on with a renewed determination to find the little yapper and get home to her fire, wine and book.

Zazoo was one of the major prizes in Arlena's latest breakup. She'd won custody of him after her split from Vance Reynolds, the A-list movie star. Arlena and Vance dated for less than two years, but that was long enough for her to net some serious time in the celebrity big leagues, walking red carpets, going to parties and vacationing in all the right places. Arlena was devastated when they split, especially since Vance wasted no time making a fresh start with a new leading lady. She insisted on keeping Zazoo, who they had picked out together when he was a puppy. Vance agreed willingly, mostly because he was headed off to a film set in Istanbul and couldn't take Zazoo along. They'd yet to work out any visitation arrangements.

Penelope reluctantly trudged on a half-mile farther and was considering giving up her search when a lump in the snow up ahead caught her eye.

"Oh no," she said under her breath. A fuzzy white puff lay motionless beneath a tree in the plowed up bank of snow at the edge of the golf course.

"Crap."

Penelope looked back towards the house but Arlena was out of sight. She stood for a moment, staring at the mound in the snow, willing it to move. Or better yet waiting for her eyes to re-focus and realize it was just a plop of snow fallen from the tree and not the dead body of Arlena's beloved dog. After a few moments of squinting and trying to make out the figure, she decided it definitely hadn't moved at all since she noticed it.

Penelope sighed and pulled her knit cap farther down on her head. She walked closer to the tree to get a better look, wishing the whole time that she had been the one to turn back towards home. She hated the idea of finding Zazoo, dead or injured, and breaking Arlena's already fragile heart.

The closer she got the more convinced she was that she was seeing the lifeless body of Zazoo, the spunky little dog who would launch himself straight up in the air over and over whenever he was happy to see someone. Penelope had never had a dog of her own but she felt she shared custody of Zazoo, feeding him his homemade organic diet regularly and walking him when Arlena didn't take him to the set dressed in one of his little doggie outfits.

"Zazoo?" she said, squinting and edging closer. "Come on, buddy." She moved in to investigate, the snow rising farther up her calves with each step. She pulled her boot up out of the snow to take one last large step towards the fuzzy lump. As she bounded forward, she tripped on a tree root buried beneath the snow, causing her to fall forward into the snow bank, her face almost landing on top of the semi-buried dog.

"Ugh!" She scrambled to get up, her thin pants soaking up the freezing moisture like a dry sponge. Her legs began to throb with the cold almost instantly. As she struggled to stand up, she slipped again, landing once more into the snow and onto something hard.

"Great," she sighed, shaking her head. She took a deep breath and reached out her soaking wet mitten to grab the dog. As she pulled, she realized too late that what she grabbed was way too light. Her arm did an exaggerated yank straight up into the air, a white puff waving at the top of her arm.

"Oh my God. Help! Help!" Penelope screamed horror-movie style, filling the cold night air and the space between her ears with a jangling chorus. She did not recognize her own voice as it bounced off of the trees into the dark nothingness just beyond. "Help!" Penelope felt her throat closing up, tightening against her cries. She lay rigid and helpless in the snow, unable to move.

Arlena came running down the road, the beam of her flashlight bouncing wildly in the dark. When she turned the bend, she saw Penelope lying face down in a snow bank, soaking wet and screaming, waving a fluffy white ski cap in the air, her face inches away from that of a dead girl's.

CHAPTER 2

Arlena and Penelope sat next to each other and shivered, both from the cold and from the shock of finding a dead girl buried in the snow outside their house. They sat on stools behind the black granite-topped kitchen island, grasping mugs of hot chocolate and shaking under the big blankets that the brusque female police officer had draped over their shoulders.

Zazoo jumped straight up in the air in the kitchen between the three of them, yapping happily.

"You were out walking your dog?" Officer Jenkins asked them. Her bottle blond hair was slicked against her skull and wrapped in a tight bun at the base of her muscular neck. She had an orange tan and smelled like cocoa butter and sea salt. Penelope glanced at the opaque white skin on her own hands, the blue veins at her wrists.

"No," Arlena sighed, her exasperation peeking through her practiced, patient public persona. "He had run off, and we were out looking for him."

"Uh-huh." Officer Jenkins made a note in her leather bound flip pad, her French manicured nails clicking against the pen. "And you two are what? Roommates? Girlfriends?" She did not look up from her pad.

Arlena rolled her eyes. "Penelope is my personal chef, and

my friend. And we're currently working together on the same film in South Point."

"Your dog was here the whole time you guys were out looking for him?" Officer Jenkins said, still scribbling furiously. Her gaze bounced between the two women.

Penelope cut her eyes sideways at Arlena.

"Yes," Arlena said. "No, I mean, he had run off, but when we came back here to call you he was waiting at the back door."

"That's when the lights came back on," Penelope offered, her voice still raspy from the cold, and from screaming. She stared into her mug, watching the foam cloud on top of her chocolate change shape. She had drunk almost half of the warm liquid but realized she didn't remember tasting anything. Her mouth was as dry as cardboard.

"And you've never seen the young girl outside before?" Officer Jenkins asked. Her eyes never rested in one place for very long, so it was hard for them to figure out who she was talking to.

"I only saw a little of her, part of her face was sticking out of the snow and she was so blue." A shiver came over Penelope as she pictured the full blue lips on the girl's frozen face. "But no, I don't think so. We work on movie sets and we see hundreds of people a day, a lot of them strangers if they're extras or day players."

The radio on Officer Jenkins' shoulder lapel chirped loudly. Arlena and Penelope both jumped as if someone had slammed the door. Zazoo yelped and trotted over to his little red doggie bed in the corner of the kitchen, folding himself down gently onto the cushion. He had finally stopped barking, but he still kept his eyes trained on the action in the room.

"Detective Baglioni is here," announced a windblown male voice on her shoulder. It was one of the uniformed officers milling around outside.

"Perfect. Detective Baglioni is here," she muttered. "Roger that," she said to her shoulder as she pressed the button on the side of the radio. Penelope noticed Officer Jenkins had quite a bicep under her brown uniform shirt. And if she wasn't mistaken, fake boobs. The woman obviously spent a lot of time at the gym. And the tanning salon, based on the orange glow of her skin.

"Okay, ladies. Thank you for your statements. The detective will have some questions for you, I'm sure," Officer Jenkins said. Her frosted pink lips settled into a tight line on her tanned face, creating two sets of parentheses beside her mouth. Penelope wondered if the woman ever smiled. She certainly hadn't in front of them, even during her half-hearted attempts at comforting them.

"More questions? I don't know if I can. We both have early calls tomorrow and—"

"It won't take long, Miss Madison. We appreciate your cooperation," Officer Jenkins said, a tone of finality in her voice.

Arlena sighed and leaned closer to Penelope, shrugging farther under the blanket over her shoulders and crossing her arms tightly across her chest.

Zazoo stood up on his bed and let out a series of excited yaps, the bark he reserved for anyone he didn't know who came into the house. Detective Baglioni strode into the kitchen, glancing all around the room, looking everywhere but at the two women sitting behind the granite topped kitchen island.

"Hello, Detective," Officer Jenkins said, looking at the floor. Her hands were clasped tightly behind her back and she rocked gently on her steel-toed boots.

"Jenkins," the man replied.

Penelope saw his eyes move across her face and noticed the slight upturn of a smile on his lips. She got the sense of familiarity there, beyond them just passing each other in a squad room. Detective Baglioni had deep green eyes with gold flecks in them, set slightly close on his face, a strong jaw bone and a perfect nose, like the ones she'd seen on marble statues at the Met. A hint of stubble brushed his chin and Penelope absently rubbed her cheek as he spoke.

"Thank you for taking the time to speak with us, ladies. I'm Detective Joseph Baglioni." He addressed Arlena first and then he glanced at Penelope, pausing a beat to study her face. Something about the detective rang a distant bell with Penelope, but she couldn't quite place it.

"Is there anything you can think of beyond what you've told Officer Jenkins?"

Penelope glanced sideways at Arlena, who was shaking her head. "I don't think so."

A muscle twitched in his jaw and he glanced behind them at the dark wood cabinets.

"What happened to that girl? Did she get hit by a car or run over by a snow plow?" Arlena asked.

Penelope put an arm around Arlena's shoulders, worried she might get hysterical again like she did when they first found the girl. And then again when they got home and were trying to get themselves together to call the police, fumbling with the alarm and their phones and trying to quiet Zazoo's torrent of barking.

Tears crowded the corners of Arlena's eyes.

"Maybe. But there's no sign of an accident, no fresh tire marks leading to or from the snow bank. Of course a plow might have wiped any evidence of them away. It looks like she may have suffered a blow to the head. Do either of you recognize the girl from the neighborhood?"

Arlena and Penelope shook their heads again. The welling tears flopped out of Arlena's eyes and down her cheeks in pretty little streams. Penelope always marveled at how Arlena looked beautiful even when she cried. When Penelope cried, it was all red-faced and messy, definitely not film-worthy.

"You're saying someone might have attacked that girl out on our street and then left her out there to die in the cold? Does that mean it's dangerous to be in our neighborhood right now?" Arlena's mood had shifted to indignation laced with a touch of fear. "What are you going to do about it?"

"We're doing what we can, Miss Madison. Our team is outside, processing the scene and questioning your neighbors."

"You'll let us know if for some reason we're not safe or if there is anything else we should be doing?" Penelope asked.

"Of course," he said. "You have an alarm system, so I'd advise you to keep it on at all times. If you see anyone suspicious or anything out of the ordinary, call us right away. Here's my card." He slipped two white business cards onto the island, one for each of them. "You've got a private security company that patrols this neighborhood and we'll brief them, let them know to be on the lookout and report anything suspicious. And we'll keep a presence in the neighborhood until we know what we're dealing with."

Penelope picked up his business card. "Joey Baglioni. From down the block?"

Joey smiled. "Yep, that's me, Penny Blue."

"We grew up together," Penelope said to Arlena. She couldn't believe the homicide detective standing in her kitchen was her friend and neighbor from grade school. "Wow, you're a detective now?"

He nodded. "I thought I recognized you when I first came in. It's been a while. It's good to see you, not under these circumstances of course." He cleared his throat and continued, "Please, let me know immediately if anything comes to mind or if you have any concerns."

"Thank you, Detective," Arlena said with a note of

impatience. She glanced at the clock on the oven door. "If there's nothing else, we both have to be on set very early..." She indicated the kitchen door with a flick of her dark brown eyes.

"You can reach me at that number," he said, nodding at no one in particular and heading towards the door, Officer Jenkins close behind.

CHAPTER 3

The next morning Penelope paused for a moment to watch the first streaks of sunlight cut through the morning sky before switching on the generator behind the catering tent, which served as the dining hall on the movie set. Inside, the tent was lined from end to end with collapsible eight-foot dining tables and three hundred and fifty folding chairs, empty seats waiting for cold and tired cast and crew to come and enjoy breakfast, lunch and dinner during the day's shoot. Penelope's team was responsible for keeping everyone fed and happy on time to ensure filming stayed on schedule.

Stifling a yawn, she headed to the kitchen truck parked near the tent to get the first of what she knew would be several cups of coffee. She climbed inside her custom designed food truck and slid the door closed behind her, enjoying the warmth that radiated from the two large ovens, the grated grill and flat cook-top provided. Penelope had switched everything on and made the first big urn of coffee right after she'd pulled up to the set. She filled a paper cup full of hot coffee and looked up at the menu notes above the still-shuttered service windows.

The door of the truck slid open and Francis appeared, shivering inside his thick puffy jacket. "Morning, Boss. Sorry I'm late."

Penelope looked at the digital clock next to the daily menus, which read 5:14. She'd asked her chefs to be in by five so they'd have time to get breakfast ready for everyone else who were reporting to set at seven. "What happened? You're never late."

"I had my alarm set for four, but it didn't go off. And my car was buried. Sorry, Boss."

"Did you guys loose power here in town?"

"Nah, I don't know what happened. But the clocks were working," Francis said. He poured himself a cup of coffee. "The other guys are here, I picked them up on the way. They're already in the prep tent, cutting fruit for breakfast."

"Do me a favor and get a backup alarm before you go home today, or remember to set your phone to get you up. You're going to have to hustle to get everything ready by call time."

"You got it." Francis took another big sip of coffee, put his cup down and rubbed his hands together to warm them.

"And get one of the guys to set up the craft table with cereal and juice, some granola bars, too."

"You got it. We'll be ready."

Penelope lit the charcoals underneath her omelet grill, a six-foot-long skinny basin that she could fit ten pans on at a time. Next to it was a collapsible table with glass bowls full of chopped vegetables, cheeses and meats. She could make ten omelets to order at a time as the diners filed through the line in front of her. She'd had a friend from culinary school custom-build the grill to her specifications, just the way she wanted it. It was much easier taking orders out in the open behind the grill than leaning through the window of the food truck and using the flat top grill to make omelets one at a time. She worked out in the cold this way, but efficiency had won out over comfort.

Various cast and crew members nodded and offered

mumbled greetings as they came through her line, shivering in their jackets and watching the eggs bubble up in the pans in front of them. She greeted them warmly as she prepared their omelets, grateful to be getting their long day ahead started.

When breakfast service was over and the cast and crew went to work on the morning shoot, Penelope and her chefs cleared down and began prepping for lunch. Francis, Penelope's sous-chef, was in the kitchen truck, searing off chicken breasts and filleting salmon. The rest of her team was in the adjoining tent prepping vegetables for salads and sides. The film's production company was paying a local restaurant to wash their dishes after each meal, so they only had to deliver the bus trays full of dirty dishes and pick up fresh plates and glasses before lunch, all ready to go in drying racks wrapped in plastic. While expensive, it saved her team so much time and effort. After working on a few movie sets Penelope understood the reason behind the multimillion-dollar price tags that even small movies racked up. A movie set was like a portable city, and each moving part had its own cost.

Her crew well underway with the lunch prep, Penelope decided to take a break and check in on Arlena in makeup. She grabbed an orange out of the fruit bin, lightly patting one of her chefs on his shoulder as she passed. He nodded but kept his focus on the cutting board in front of him, his sharp chef knife slicing quickly through a large red tomato. Penelope pulled off her long black apron, set it down at the edge of his station and zipped up her fleece jacket. She ducked out from under the flap of the tent and headed towards the trailers grouped at the back of South Point's municipal parking lot. The makeup, talent and wardrobe trailers were grouped together in the center of their temporary trailer park. It was an unwritten rule of every crew Penelope had worked with to set them up that way to limit the access of long range paparazzi camera lenses or every day lookie-loos who hovered near the edges of a set, hoping to catch a glimpse of someone famous.

When Penelope entered the makeup trailer, she saw Arlena reclining in a chair with cucumber slices over her eyes, her wet hair wrapped in a towel. She wore a bathrobe over silky pajamas and big fuzzy slippers, all in matching shades of blue. Kelley, the head makeup artist on the film, was sitting on a short stool at her side, massaging one of her hands. Arlena's body stiffened when she heard the door open.

"Sorry, it's me," Penelope said, closing the door quickly to keep the frosty air outside.

"Oh, hey," Arlena said, relaxing back into the chair. She pulled the cucumbers off of her eyes with her free hand.

"I brought you an orange," Penelope said.

"Thanks. Can you dip it in chocolate and deep fry it for me?" Arlena asked, laughing weakly.

"No, but I can peel it for you. You want any, Kelley?"

"Thanks, I'm fine." Kelley continued to knead Arlena's hand, gently pressing on pressure points in an attempt to reduce her stress. Kelley's hair was bright purple today and cut in a cute retro bob, Betty Boop style. She was tall and thin and her long body curved into a C when she sat down. She changed her look and hair color constantly, sometimes platinum blond, sometimes jet black. Penelope always admired people who took those fashion risks. She'd never felt that bold.

There was a knock on the door and someone yelled, "Miss Madison, I have your new pages for today. Sal just called thirty minutes." It was one of the production assistants, sent around to remind everyone when they were expected on set.

"New pages?" Arlena asked. "Sal never said anything about new pages. Pen, can you grab them for me?"

Penelope nodded and opened the door, leaning out to get the script pages from the PA. "Thanks." She closed the door quickly against the cold air and handed the pile of typed script pages to Arlena.

Arlena sighed and took an orange segment from Penelope's hand, glancing down at the sheets. "What I wouldn't give to be home in bed."

"Me too," Penelope said.

"Arlena was telling me about last night. It sounds awful." Kelley's eyes were rimmed with black liner and perfectly applied smoky grey eye shadow that created a cat's eye effect. Penelope remembered to swipe on some mascara after jumping out of the shower, but that was it for today.

"It's scary to think someone got killed right outside our home." Arlena bit into the orange segment and continued to read, shaking her head slightly. "I haven't seen any of this dialogue before...they must have written it all last night. It's the same setting we rehearsed but the words are all different."

"Will they have it on a monitor for you?" Penelope asked.

Arlena scoffed, "No. Sal doesn't believe in cue cards. He likes things to be more organic. The script supervisor will be there if I need her to call a line for me, but I know that throws everyone off. I'll have to sit with this for a bit until I get it down."

"In the next thirty minutes?" Penelope asked, alarmed for her friend. Arlena was holding at least five new pages of dialogue.

"Wish me luck," Arlena said, scanning through the words.

"I read about the girl who got killed by your house last night in the *Ledger*," Kelley said to Penelope, nodding towards the makeup table at her iPad. The *Northern New Jersey Ledger* website was pulled up on the screen, and "Teen Found Dead" was the lead story on the site.

Penelope skimmed the beginning of the article. "It says her name was Holly Anderson. Are there any Andersons on our street?"

Arlena shrugged. "I don't think so. Not that I'm aware of."

"She was only sixteen," Penelope said quietly.

Arlena shook her head. "It's terrible, isn't it? It doesn't appear they know much more than her name."

"I suppose they're still investigating whether or not it was an accident," Penelope said, scanning the rest of the article and setting the iPad back down on the makeup counter.

"That detective didn't seem to think it was an accident," Arlena said. "He didn't want to scare us by telling us that a maniac is on the loose."

Kelley got up and gently removed the towel from Arlena's head and began dragging a comb gently through her long black hair, glancing at the photos she had taped to the top of the makeup mirror. They each had a date marked on them so she would know which hairstyle Arlena required for each day's shoot. Kelley put the comb down and began blow-drying Arlena's hair, wrapping it around a round thistle brush.

"I'm heading back. We're supposed to break for lunch at one," Penelope shouted over the dryer. Penelope slipped her iPhone out of the back pocket of her jeans to check the time. It was only nine thirty but she already felt like she had worked a twelve-hour day.

"Thanks for the orange," Arlena said distractedly, still staring at the script.

Kelley mouthed "thank you" to Penelope as she left the trailer.

Penelope could always tell when the cast and crew had gone to work because the lot became very quiet, in stark contrast to when everyone was in between shoots, milling around, talking and laughing or meeting in the tent to eat. She knew the office staff was working in the production trailers, but other than that, it would be a ghost town until they finished filming. Penelope let the staff play music on the truck, as long as it didn't bother anyone else, and she found herself humming along to some of the songs as she worked, overseeing the crew while they prepared lunch.

Penelope was deboning a large slab of salmon and using her knife to portion out pieces for lunch when the two-way radio clipped to the pocket of her apron chirped. "Catering, come in?"

Penelope wiped her hands on a prep towel before grabbing the radio and responding, "This is catering, go ahead."

"Sal is requesting Penelope Sutherland report to set," the voice said.

Penelope stared at the radio for a second, trying to figure out why the director of the movie would want the head caterer on the film on set. She pressed the button and said, "Do you need the craft table refreshed? Because I can get—"

"Negative. Not a craft issue. Sal wants to see Penelope Sutherland on set right away."

Penelope looked at the radio again and back down at her salmon. She pressed the button again. "I'm on my way."

"What's up, Boss?" Francis said from behind her.

"I'm not sure. Do me a favor and finish this up? Five ounce fillets. Don't weigh them, just eyeball it."

"Sure thing," Francis said, moving to the sink to wash his hands.

Penelope walked through the lot to the warehouse that the crew was using for the interior scenes of the movie. The set designers had created several spaces inside, designed to look like various rooms or locations. She knew from talking with Arlena the night before, and from glancing at the call sheet that morning that they were downstairs in the space they'd created to look like a coffee shop.

When Penelope entered the space, the script supervisor met

her at the entryway to the coffee shop with an anxious expression on her face. "Penelope, right?" she asked quickly. When Penelope nodded she said, "What happened this morning?"

Penelope tried to figure out what she was asking. "What do you mean? Did something happen at breakfast?" She looked over the woman's shoulder and saw Arlena watching them, also looking very anxious.

The young girl thrust a stack of script pages at her, which looked like the ones she'd been handed earlier outside of Arlena's trailer. "Where did you get these?"

Penelope looked at the pages, noticing Arlena's scribbled handwriting around the edges, where she'd made notes to herself. "I didn't. One of the PAs handed them to me outside makeup."

Sal Marco walked over and Penelope's stomach dropped. He looked angry and that's when she noticed everyone on the set was staring at her, and no one else was saying a word. "Who was it?"

"I'm not sure, he was bundled up and I only leaned out for a second. He said there were new pages for Arlena, that's it." Penelope looked at Arlena and held her palms up in the air. "That's all that happened."

Sal sighed and shook his head. "Now we're behind, because someone has decided to play a prank on me. Where these lines came from I have no idea. I never approved any of these changes. It took us ten minutes to figure out why Arlena was getting all of her lines wrong. The kid behind the coffee counter with one line was doing a better job than my lead actress."

Arlena said, "Sorry, Sal."

"It's okay, we'll reset and start again." Sal turned to Penelope. "You sure you didn't recognize the guy?"

Penelope looked down at her shoes and put her hands on

her hips, trying to remember. "I didn't see his face, but if it was one of the assistants, I don't know all of them by name."

Sal stared at her and pulled the radio from his belt. Pressing the button, he said, "Have all of the interns and PAs report to set immediately." He clicked off the radio and said to Penelope, "You're going to point him out to me."

The script supervisor watched him go and then turned to give Penelope one last shrug. It was her job to maintain continuity of the story during filming, so Penelope figured she got a good talking to by Sal before they figured out what had happened.

A few minutes later Penelope eyed the line of young people in front of her.

"No one will admit to delivering those phony script pages to Arlena," Sal said. "Tell me who you saw and I'll make sure they never set foot on another movie set."

After walking up and down twice in front of them, Penelope said, "I can't tell. It doesn't look like any of them. He was taller, I think."

Sal sighed, blowing out some frustration. "We've wasted enough time on this already. Let's take five and start again." He looked at Arlena. "Let's do the scene like we originally rehearsed."

Arlena nodded eagerly and the script supervisor rushed over, handing her what Penelope assumed were the correct script pages to refresh her memory.

Sal turned to Penelope. "You can go."

CHAPTER 4

It was almost lunchtime the following day and Penelope was chopping flat leaf parsley to garnish a large tray of beautifully roasted salmon. She arranged lemon wedges around the edges of the tray and sprinkled the parsley, pressing on the fillets here and there with her finger to test for doneness. She had pulled one off to taste before plating them and she knew that they were perfect: medium rare and crispy on the outside. The kitchen truck smelled of roasted salmon, potatoes and fresh herbs, one of the best smells on earth, as far as Penelope was concerned.

"These are ready," she said to Francis. He knelt down so his shoulder was level with the steel countertop and slid the tray onto it. He stood up and headed out of the kitchen truck and into the catering tent to place the fish on the serving table where the first of the crew had already lined up. They were also serving lemon and herb roasted chicken and veggie lasagna accompanied with roasted butternut squash, new potatoes with rosemary, wild rice and mushrooms and Brussels sprouts roasted with garlic. As always there were five cold salads to choose from including arugula and goat cheese, mixed baby greens, an Italian salad with Romaine lettuce, radicchio, and plain old iceberg for those crew members who preferred a basic salad.

Penelope walked up and down behind the long food tables

as the guests came through, serving themselves from the steam tables and iced down salad bar. She loved watching the reactions of the diners when they saw her food for the first time. She had to admit it was fun to see what her more famous guests thought, the actors, directors and producers, but she also loved cooking for the teamsters, carpenters, grips and production office employees.

"Good job, Penelope." Sal had noticed her behind the line as he came back over for seconds.

"Thanks, Sal. Glad you enjoyed it," Penelope said. "Do you have any requests this week? Maybe I can make up for what happened earlier."

"Sal, don't make her do any extra work," a thin blond woman strolled up behind him, her plate piled high with fresh spinach and a few strawberries.

Sal waved his hand at her. "This is my wife, Paige."

"Oh, it's nice to meet you, Mrs. Marco," Penelope said.

"You too. Thanks for lunch," Paige added before popping a strawberry into her mouth and walking to one of the dining tables. She had a dog-eared paperback tucked under her arm with different colored sticky notes marking various pages. "Sal, I made some notes on dialogue I wanted to show you."

He nodded at her quickly and then turned his attention back to Penelope. "You think you could do Italian one night? Maybe on Friday, kind of a celebration of our first week finished?"

"Sure. Let me work out a menu."

"I know you can cook. Hopefully you can make a nice marinara for us." He scooped some baby red potatoes onto his plate next to his second helping of chicken.

A faint police siren sounded in the distance, which wasn't unusual in New Jersey on any given day, but after all of the police activity in her life recently, Penelope tilted her ear towards it. The radio hooked onto Penelope's back pocket and the one clipped to Sal's belt both came to life at once. One of the production assistants spoke nervously over the crackling walkie-talkie.

"On set EMT has been called to Main Street location. There's been an accident. One of the principals is down."

A crowd ran from the lot towards picturesque Main Street in South Point, New Jersey. Large spotlights up on tall stands and a tent set up for Sal's team blocked the sidewalk. Traffic had been diverted from the street during a three-hour window that day for the crew. Several members of the crew milled around nervously in the middle of the street, but they were all looking in the same general direction.

Penelope ran alongside Sal who kept saying "Are you kidding me? Oh shit." He was squeezing the radio tight in his fist, his knuckles white against his thick red fingers.

Penelope could see a group of people gathered around someone lying on the ground in the middle of the street. She tried to see who it was through the various arms and legs blocking her view.

"It's Arlena," Sal said hurriedly, picking up his pace.

Penelope sped up, shoving her way past a few crew members standing by one of the cameras. She vaguely noticed a group of onlookers standing on the curb on the other side of the traffic barricades, gawking at all of the activity. A few of them had their phones out, recording the scene. The movie cameras were in position but it didn't look like they were rolling.

"Arlena!" Penelope shouted as she made her way to her friend lying prone in the street, her head propped up on a crumpled tan blazer. Penelope's heart thudded through her sweater and her legs had turned rubbery. Sam Cavanaugh, the famous actor and Arlena's co-star, was holding Arlena's hand. Penelope could tell from his matching pants that it was his suit jacket wadded into a ball under her head. He was on his knees, his face inches from Arlena's, whispering softly to her as she lay motionless, her legs and arms flat on the pavement. On the other side of Arlena were the movie's two on-set EMTs. The lead EMT, a tiny woman with blond hair, was holding up Arlena's eyelid and shining a small flashlight at her pupil.

"What the hell happened?" Sal shouted.

Several members of the crew stepped forward and started talking at once.

"Came out of nowhere..."

"...mowed her down from behind..."

"...she didn't see him coming...her head hit the ground..."

The lead EMT brushed her bangs out of her eyes with the back of her latex-gloved hand. "Bring me a long board and a cervical collar," she said to her assistant. He jumped up and hurried to the ambulance, grabbing the items she requested. When he returned, she took the collar from him and carefully placed it around Arlena's neck. Then the two of them moved her onto the narrow board, being careful not to jostle her. Sam released Arlena's hand right before they hoisted her up and rolled her into the back of the idling ambulance. Sal and Penelope stood by his side, Sal resting a hand on Sam's shoulder.

"We're taking her to the Medical Center over on Baker Street. Want to rule out a concussion," the EMT said. "She has a welt here, probably the point of impact." She indicated a place just above her own hairline. "Could be only a bad fall but when they lose consciousness, we have to check them out to be safe."

Sal nodded. Penelope felt sick to her stomach and didn't quite trust her legs to stay steady. "Should I go with her?"

The EMT shook her head. "It's not necessary. We're taking

precautions. She'll probably have a bad headache and a bump on her head. Like I said, I'd like the doctor to rule out anything more serious." With that she turned on her heel and climbed into the back of the ambulance. Her assistant shut the door behind her and jogged over to the driver's side door, hopped inside and quickly drove away with Penelope's best friend and Sal's leading lady tucked away inside.

"Christ. I cannot believe this is happening today," Sal yelled, letting his anger overtake his worry. He spun around to glare at the mostly silent crew, still gathered in a loose huddle near the scene of the accident. Penelope and Sam stood dazed where the ambulance had been. Sam's face was white underneath his tan camera makeup and he twisted his crumpled jacket in his fists.

"Sam, what happened?" Sal asked him, turning back to his leading man, grasping his muscular bicep. Sal spoke gently, trying to shake Sam from his shock and get him to focus.

"Ah, um..." Sam searched for words, not looking directly at them but all around instead, like he was trying to find his words on invisible cue cards. "We were running lines, walking our cues and then," he drifted for a second, "and then she got run over by a golf cart. It's crazy because I heard it speed up behind us right before..."

"Who was it?" Sal urged.

Sam held his palms up. "I didn't see a face, whoever it was had on a ski mask, and the back window was covered with something, like black plastic, maybe a garbage bag, so I couldn't see after they passed."

"Someone ran over my leading lady and no one knows who it was?" Sal was shouting again now. "Do you know how much money this is costing me?"

The crew members seemed to shrink, shoulders sagging as they glanced at each other for an answer.

"You," Sal waved over the Key Grip.

A thin man in a puffy jacket reluctantly walked over to Sal.

"You were hanging the camera?" Sal waved at a small crane on the other side of the street that held a camera, rigged to film a tracking shot.

The grip nodded, screwing up his blond features. "Yeah, Sal, but I didn't see what happened. It was over in two seconds...I saw the cart hauling out of here. It was one of ours, though, that I know for sure."

"How did you not see what happened? You had a bird's-eye view of the street." Sal paced angrily back and forth, clenching his fists. "The barricades are up. They were rehearsing, the street was cleared of traffic and there was no one else around. And what? Someone decided to drive through my movie? Not only that, but drive through and hit my lead actress and not even stop to see if she's been injured?"

"I'm sorry, Sal," the grip said. "I wish I could tell you what happened." He glanced at his fellow crew mates, most of who were attempting not to make eye contact with him.

Sal laughed darkly, shaking his head. "You know what? If Arlena is not back here one hundred percent fine and ready to work tomorrow, I'm holding all of you personally responsible." Sal stomped away angrily from his crew.

"Sam, are you okay?" Penelope asked, raising a hand to touch his shoulder but pulling back at the last minute.

Sam looked at her, still dazed. "I guess so."

"Do you think someone did this on purpose?"

Sam nodded quickly. "I heard the cart speed up, and then they went even faster to get away. Didn't stop or hesitate once."

Penelope's stomach did a slow turn. "Someone on the set, then," she mumbled to herself. "Someone was aiming for her."

CHAPTER 5

"Ouch. Ouch. Ouch."

Penelope could hear Arlena's voice coming from a room at the end of the hall. They were on the top floor of South Point Medical Center, in the most private room the facility could offer. The rubber soles of her Doc Marten boots squished against the linoleum floor as she made her way through the quiet hallway towards room 608. She had Arlena's large Marc Jacobs tote bag slung over one shoulder and her long black coat draped over her arm. She'd grabbed them both from Arlena's trailer before she'd left for the hospital.

"Ouch!" Arlena said once again. Penelope poked her head into the room and saw a short Indian man in a white coat pressing gently on Arlena's scalp in different places. A plastic badge that read Dr. Amit Singh was clipped to his jacket pocket. Arlena's shiny black hair was fanned out on the pillow and she had dark red lipstick on. If Penelope hadn't known about the accident she might think Arlena was filming a scene for a medical drama on Lifetime.

"Miss Madison, you're going to be fine," Dr. Singh said. "I'm releasing you back to work tomorrow. I'd like you to go home now and rest until then." His voice was soft and had a soothing lyrical quality to it.

"But we're filming until eight tonight and it's—"

"Tomorrow, Miss Madison. I don't want you to run the risk of falling if you become dizzy and faint. You could reinjure yourself. Rest now and you'll get better sooner." He gave Arlena a stern look. His phone began to buzz in his pocket and he pulled it out to glance at the screen.

"I can take you home," Penelope said from the doorway.

Doctor Singh glanced up at Penelope. "Good. You will take her home and make sure she rests. No disco clubs tonight."

Penelope laughed. "Only tonight, we'll stay out of the disco clubs."

"Thank goodness you're here," Arlena said, sighing gratefully.

"Arlena." Sam Cavanaugh, her onscreen husband, came rushing through the door, bumping Penelope into the door frame in the process.

"Sam. What are you doing here?" Arlena's hands instinctively went to her hair and face, checking to make sure she was brushed and made up. She glanced at Penelope, silently pleading with her to confirm she was presentable. Not just normal presentable, but a-handsome-man-is-near presentable. Penelope gave her a subtle thumbs up from the doorway, and Arlena's shoulders relaxed back onto the bed.

"I was so worried. Also, they wrapped for the day. They need both of us to do our scenes together," he said. He took Arlena's hand and tucked her hair behind her ear in one fluid motion, practiced and natural. "You're here and I was there, so I came here. I can't stop seeing the image of you flying through the air, landing on your head. That was crazy."

Maybe Sam was still in shock from witnessing the accident. She glanced at Arlena, but she was smiling at him, apparently unaware of his rambling. Doctor Singh stared at Sam, his mouth frozen in a silent O.

"Dr. Reynolds," Dr. Singh exclaimed.

Sam had gotten his big break a few years ago playing Dr. Jonathan Reynolds on *Emergency*, a must-see hospital drama on TV. Penelope wondered if the doctors and nurses at South Point Medical Center were walking around half naked and having sex in the supply closets downstairs. Probably not. She hadn't seen anyone as good looking as Sam Cavanaugh or any of his costars down there. Not by a long shot.

"Yep, that's me," Sam said.

"Can I get a picture? I'm a big fan," Dr. Singh said.

"Sure, anything for Arlena's doctor." He moved around to Dr. Singh's side of the bed.

The doctor held his phone up in the air and tried to throw his arm around Sam's shoulders. Sam was at least a foot taller than the doctor, and the shorter man's arm didn't quite reach. He settled for looping an arm around Sam's waist. He snapped the picture from his upraised hand as they both smiled at the phone.

"That was my favorite show during my residency. I never missed an episode. When you died of cancer, I couldn't believe it. The show wasn't ever the same after that," Dr. Singh said, shaking his head.

Penelope remembered Sam being a very robust, healthy-looking cancer patient, still sexy with his shaved head, breaking the hearts of both the ambitious young doctor and the long-suffering ex-girlfriend nurse who loved him. He eventually died in the nurse's arms, scoring a ratings high for the show.

"It's right in here." Penelope heard a woman's voice from behind her in the hallway. A nurse was showing Detective Baglioni into Arlena's tiny room. He squeezed through the doorway, brushing Penelope as he went.

"Excuse me, Miss Sutherland."

Penelope's cheeks flushed and it took her a minute to

refocus on the adult conversation in the room. Now there were three men in Arlena's room surrounding her narrow hospital bed, a modern day Snow White and three Prince Charmings, each hoping to plant a kiss and win her heart forever.

"Hello, Arlena, Doctor. And..." He looked at Sam, waiting for an introduction.

"Sam Cavanaugh."

"Oh yeah, Jack Sloan."

One of Sam's best known movie roles was action hero Jack Sloan. He saved the world every two to three years up on the big screen chasing terrorists, disabling bombs, landing burning airplanes and diverting rogue missiles, most of the time in a shredded shirt or a tight bathing suit. He usually started out in Armani but would end up in the buff with a constantly revolving list of leading ladies, the world safe once again. Penelope figured Arlena would do anything to be in a Jack Sloan movie.

"I must go and check on another patient," Dr. Singh said. "Call me if you have any concerns, Arlena." He turned and made his way through the crowded room. He brushed past Penelope, still standing in the doorway, on his way out. The room had become overheated and Penelope unzipped her puffy jacket.

"Thanks, Doctor," Arlena called after him. Sam took the seat beside Arlena's bed and placed her hand gently in his. Penelope briefly wondered if he remembered he was her husband in the movie, not in real life. Maybe he was staying in character on and off the set like Daniel Day-Lewis or Viggo Mortensen.

"Someone gave you a bump on the head, huh?" Detective Baglioni asked. He glanced at the monitors on the wall over Arlena's head.

"How did you know?"

"I was downstairs questioning a stabbing victim and heard the nurses buzzing about you being up here," he said.

"Wow, a stabbing?" Penelope asked.

Joey nodded tightly at her and turned back to Arlena.

"I was in an accident on the set. Someone from the crew wasn't watching where they were going and ran me over with a golf cart. At least that's what I've been told. I don't really remember."

"So you were, what? Running down the street? Or you were behind something and he didn't see you?"

"No, we were rehearsing a sidewalk dialogue scene. Sam and me." She squeezed Sam's hand and he nodded at her. "In the scene we're window shopping, looking for presents for our adopted son...the one I pushed Sam to adopt but he had reservations about because the boy is a war refugee from Sudan. It's a very powerful scene, a real turning point in the movie. We wanted to run it together a few times before Sal came for the day's shoot."

"I see, so definitely not a car chase," Joey said.

"No, there aren't any car chases in *Remember the Fall*. It's an art film about a marriage coming apart at the seams," Arlena explained patiently.

"Ah, a date night flick." He chuckled, glancing at Penelope. "I thought you stuck to the action flicks, Mr. Cavanaugh."

"You have to *stretch* as an artist, so..." Sam trailed off, gazing at Arlena. Penelope remembered hearing Sam say that in an interview on *Access Hollywood*, back when he made the transition from TV to film.

"That's true, Sam. So true," Arlena said, returning his gaze. "They're releasing me now. Pen is here to take me home."

"Oh, I can take you," Sam said. He was still gazing into her eyes, then did the hair tuck behind her ear thing again. "I want to be sure you get there okay and that you're safe."

Penelope wondered again if she had missed something, and if Sam and Arlena were actually dating. She knew she'd never seen him at the house before. They'd only been filming *Remember the Fall* for a week, so essentially they had just met.

"Oh, Sam, thank you," Arlena breathed gratefully. "That would be wonderful." She gathered herself together, easing herself off the hospital bed.

She was still wearing her slim black trousers and tight pink sweater from earlier when the accident happened. The arm of her sweater was ripped, but it would be covered by her coat. Penelope knew Arlena would never head out in torn clothes in case the paparazzi lurked nearby. Sam put his arm around her tiny waist and helped her up from the bed.

"If Sam is taking you home, I'll head back to set and wrap up the crew, do my orders," she said, stepping into the room and handing Arlena's coat and bag to Sam.

"That sounds perfect. I'll see you later."

Penelope had seen that look before. Arlena was going to recover at home with the help of Sam's sexy Dr. Reynolds, back from the dead for an encore performance. She figured her recovery would probably include wine and candles.

"There's some crab dip in the fridge," Penelope offered.

"Sounds amazing. See you later on tonight?" Arlena asked.

"Yep. See you later," Penelope said.

Point taken. She would stay out for a while and let nature takes its course at home. Depending on how well things went, she might want to take herself out to dinner and a movie to give them as much time as possible. Sam guided Arlena carefully through the room and after a few steps she seemed to regain her balance. Arlena tossed her hair over her shoulder and said goodbye to Joey as they passed, Sam holding her purse and coat for her as he led her away.

"Are there any more developments in Holly's case?" Penelope asked once she and Joey were the only two left in the once crowded room.

"We're following up on some leads, questioning the girl's family. None of your neighbors heard or saw anything, the ones we've been able to talk to anyway."

"It was a good night to be indoors," Penelope said. She was momentarily distracted by the little gold flecks in his green irises.

"We're still determining what happened exactly. It's hard to tell anything with all the snow. It was all churned up like a herd of Clydesdales had tromped through it." He glanced at his watch.

"I'm sorry I messed up your crime scene," Penelope said quietly, slightly miffed at his comment. Although Penelope was an athletic size six, she sometimes felt a sharp contrast in comparison to Arlena, who was a tall and wispy size two and looked like a strong wind could pick her up and blow her down the street like a piece of newspaper. No woman wants to be compared to a giant horse, even in a flattering way, which this was not.

"I know it wasn't intentional." Detective Baglioni chuckled. "You were scared."

Penelope crossed her arms against her chest and leveled her gaze at him.

"You were never scared back in school. You were the bravest girl on the playground. That's how I remember you at least," Joey said.

"Luckily there were no dead bodies to trip over back in third grade," Penelope said, softening a bit. "Where did you go to school after Immaculate Heart?"

"St. Joseph's High and then right into the police academy," Joey said. St. Joseph's was an all boy's Catholic school on the north end of the town where they grew up. "You?"

"I went to the public high school in Freehold. They have a culinary arts program there. Made it easier to apply for culinary school when I graduated. I didn't have to work the line in a restaurant first, like most first years do."

"That's Penny Blue, always the planner," Joey said with a quiet laugh. "You didn't know anyone there, though, right?"

Penelope nodded, gazing at a spot over his shoulder. "No. No one from our school went there. But it worked out. I adapted, made a couple of friends in my cooking courses."

"That's brave, going to a new high school in a different town. At least some of the guys at Joseph's were from Immaculate Heart. I don't think I could've started over with new friends back then."

Penelope glanced away from his gaze. She remembered Joey from grade school, likeable and funny, but shunned by some of their classmates for being overweight. She and Joey had sat next to each other in math class in fifth grade, and she knew he got in trouble a couple of times by trying to make her laugh during the lecture, the stern priest making him copy times tables on the chalkboard in front of the class as punishment.

"I should be going," Joey said, somewhat reluctantly. He brushed past her as he left the room, glancing briefly back at her over his shoulder as he went.

Penelope watched him walk down the hallway and tried to forget how good he smelled. Like sandalwood and cinnamon gum.

❧ CHAPTER 6

Penelope drove slowly up her street, coming to a stop at the stone pillars that anchored the long driveway leading up to their house. She blew out a noisy sigh and hoped she had given Sam and Arlena enough time alone. After the hospital she had gone back to the set where her crew was finishing the dinner cleanup, breaking down steam tables and putting the kitchen and pantry trucks back in order. Penelope insisted the crew clean and arrange everything for the next day at the end of each shoot. Experience had taught her there was nothing worse than starting off the filming day disorganized. It always put them too far behind to comfortably keep up.

Before heading home, Penelope made her produce and fish orders for the next day's deliveries, signed off on payroll in the production trailer, and picked up the following day's call sheet. After her work was finished, she went to South Point's Main Street Wine Bar and had a big glass of Pinot Noir and some butternut squash soup with crusty bread for dinner to kill time.

She ate at a small table for two near the big picture windows, making notes and sketching out future menu plans in a spiral notebook. Although she was exhausted she enjoyed the peace and quiet, the good food and wine. The small votive candle on her table flickered whenever a member of the wait staff walked by. She found herself watching them, judging how they were working as if they were her own staff. She forced her mind to relax again and took another sip of wine.

Penelope thought back to when she and Arlena had met and become friends on a movie set a few years ago. Arlena was the lead actress and Penelope was one of the chefs on the catering crew. The film was *Slash 'Em Dead Again!*—the fourth installment in the *Slash 'Em!* movie series. Arlena was the top screamer, running from the terrible Slash 'Em monster for most of the movie. The movies were a huge success, terrified moviegoers eagerly lining up to pay their hard earned money to watch Arlena and other young actors and actresses chased, slashed, skewered and otherwise traumatized on the big screen.

Penelope was assigned to take care of Arlena's long list of culinary requests on the set: no fat, no processed food, no fruit after two o'clock, six coconut waters chilled in her trailer every morning, nothing containing sugar allowed anywhere near her plate, and the biggest one, absolutely no shellfish. Arlena also requested a fresh vegetable tray every morning in her trailer, and a protein shake every day at three. It was a long list of do's and don'ts, but Penelope happily prepared her meals to order and catered to every request, excited to be working on her first big movie.

Penelope's dream was to own her own on set catering business, and when she graduated from culinary school she took every theatrical job she could. She'd catered commercials for one day, rehearsals for an Off-Broadway production that closed down after one week, and a low budget music video where they director tried to pay her with gift cards. But she'd persevered through the bad jobs and put aside all of the money she could, saving up to buy her own trucks and hire a crew to launch Red Carpet Catering. *Slash 'Em Dead Again!* was the last financial boost she needed.

"You're the only one around here who doesn't make me crazy," Arlena said through tears one morning as Penelope delivered the vegetable plate to her trailer.

Penelope looked around and realized she was the only one in the trailer, and that Arlena, who had never spoken directly to her before, was talking about her. "Me?" Penelope said with disbelief.

"Yes," Arlena said, frustrated. "You listen to what I ask, you take it seriously and you do it without giving me an attitude. Or asking me a million questions." She snagged a cherry tomato from the chilled vegetable plate Penelope was holding. She pulled her lips apart in an exaggerated grimace as she bit into the tomato, trying to not smudge her thick coat of lipstick. "What was your name again?"

"Penelope Sutherland. I've enjoyed working with you," Penelope said. She placed the plate on Arlena's vanity table.

Arlena didn't respond. She paced the length of the trailer, wringing her hands and muttering quietly. Penelope knew from that day's call sheet that day Arlena was filming "the scene," her toughest one of the week. She had to lay bare her feelings and beg for her life in front of Slash 'Em, a bigger than life, scary masked psychopath. A monster who always struck at night when the actresses were all half-naked. She figured Arlena was getting into character.

"I should get back to work. Let me know if you need anything else, Miss Madison," Penelope said to Arlena's back. When she didn't turn around or respond, Penelope stepped quietly to the door.

Arlena spun towards her suddenly. "Would you come and be my chef? I could use someone like you...someone I can trust who will be there for me, keep things together for me at home."

"Wow," Penelope said, surprised at the sudden offer. She thought for a moment. "I'm not sure I'd be able to. I'm planning on starting my own theatrical catering business...it's been my dream for a long time."

"Why can't you do both? Come be my live-in chef, cook for me when I'm home. You get your company set up, I won't get in the way of that...and I'll be sure to request you on my future projects. I get what I ask for a lot of the time." Arlena ran her hands through her hair as she walked to the vanity table. She picked up a slice of cucumber and popped it into her mouth.

Penelope did some quick math in her head, thinking about the money she'd saved and her current income from the movie. If she could reduce her living expenses by moving in with Arlena, and get paid to cook for her on top of it, she could get her company off of the ground much quicker than she'd originally planned.

"When would you like me to start?" Penelope said.

Penelope packed up her tiny apartment in two days and moved into Arlena's renovated brick mansion in Glendale, New Jersey. Penelope had never lived in a town where all the houses were beautiful and neighbors gathered regularly for dinner at the country club. She'd never considered her family poor, but she did grow up on the rougher side of the tracks. Arlena's street was usually quiet, populated by domestic divas and their professional husbands who commuted into Manhattan, only forty minutes away by train. Penelope's favorite room in the house, after the sleek and well-appointed kitchen, was the library with its oversized stone fireplace. She loved cuddling up under a blanket to read or watch a movie in there whenever she had an evening off.

So far their arrangement had worked. Arlena's impulsiveness and Penelope's more reserved nature meshed well together, and Penelope liked having someone to cook for.

There was more than enough room at the house for Arlena and Penelope to live without crowding each other. Sometimes Penelope ended up doing more than just cook for Arlena, but Red Carpet Catering was thriving, so she didn't have any complaints.

Penelope's eyelids were heavy as she pulled her black Range Rover up the driveway and around the side of the house. A bright yellow Hummer, which Penelope assumed was Sam's, was parked in the front. She pulled her truck slowly into the far bay of the three car garage next to Arlena's BMW. Production provided a car service for her to and from the set, and she hardly ever drove.

Pressing the button on her visor to lower the garage door behind her, she sighed and decided she would slip quietly in through the kitchen door at the back of the house so as not to disturb Arlena and Sam. She looped her black leather messenger bag over her shoulder and followed the stone path that led from the garage through the back garden. Penelope was thankful that when the landscapers came to plow the driveway they'd remembered to clear the paths to the house.

Penelope peeked through the glass window panes of the kitchen door and didn't see anyone inside except Zazoo, dozing on his bed in the corner. She opened the door and slipped inside, thinking she would grab a wine glass and a nice bottle of red and head to the library, hopefully unnoticed, where she could unwind with her book before bed. Zazoo's head shot up and a small yip stuck in his throat when he heard the door open. Penelope made eye contact with him and put her finger to her lips, silently requesting that he stay put and be quiet. He reluctantly laid his head back down on his paws, keeping his eyes trained on her as she came inside and closed the door.

Arlena and Sam had a seven a.m. call time in the morning and it was after nine already. She figured whatever party was happening here would be ending soon. Neither of them would want to look puffy-eyed on camera.

She grabbed a bottle of Pinot out of the wine rack in the pantry and headed over to the hanging wine glasses next to the refrigerator. As she reached for a glass, she heard the low murmur of voices and muffled male grunts coming from the hallway leading to Arlena's side of the house.

"Great," Penelope whispered to herself, rolling her eyes. She grabbed the glass, tucked the wine bottle under her arm and tiptoed towards the opposite hallway and the library.

Sam's grunting stopped and then Penelope heard Arlena start up with her own grunts.

Penelope didn't want to eavesdrop on Arlena in the throes of passion with Sam Cavanaugh, even accidentally. She'd watched Sam make love many times, with lots of ladies, up on the big screen, she and millions of movie lovers everywhere. But it was creepy in real life.

She had almost made it to the doorway when she heard Sam call out, "That's it! Just like that. Now eight more."

"Eight more? Eight more what?" Penelope whispered to herself. Realizing that she needed a wine key to open her bottle, she debated heading back into the kitchen to get one. She also considered dropping her plans entirely and heading back out the door, getting into her car and driving to the nearest hotel. But then she remembered they lived in a huge house with lots of rooms and this was her home too. She resolved to grab the wine key as quickly as possible and make a break for the library.

She crept back into the kitchen, wobbling on her tiptoes. She eased open a drawer on the center kitchen island and grabbed a wine key, easing the drawer closed. Arlena shouted "Yes!" Penelope jumped and lost her grip on the opener. It fell, clattering to the wooden floor and skittering over to Zazoo's bed. He eyed Penelope suspiciously, a gravely growl in his throat, threatening a torrent of barking. She froze in place, not sure which way to go or what to do. She hoped the amorous couple hadn't heard her.

"Penelope? Is that you?" Arlena called from down the hall.

"Sorry! I dropped the wine key. It's me, no big deal. Don't get up." She rolled her eyes at herself. She stood frozen in place, wine bottle tucked under her arm, glass in hand and Zazoo at red alert.

Arlena and Sam came into the kitchen, both of them dressed in workout clothes.

"You're home," Arlena said, hugging Penelope. She was sweaty, but it was Arlena's version of sweaty: beautiful and dewy accompanied by a sweet, clean soap smell. She would never allow herself to smell like a gym locker.

"I hope I'm not interrupting anything..." Penelope said, relaxing a bit.

Sam opened the fridge and grabbed two bottles of water. He handed one to Arlena and twisted the cap off of the other one for himself. There was a sweat ring around the neck of his shirt and his biceps were shiny. Penelope admired all of the different muscles standing out so clearly on his arms and the way his shirt stretched across his chest.

"Of course not. Sam was showing me the latest moves he learned on location in Taiwan. Super killer workout, Pilates and Martial Arts mixed together." Arlena's feet were bare and perfectly shaped, her toe polish a deep rose color. She leaned into Sam and they both drank from their water bottles, arms entwined.

"It's good stuff," Sam said, running a hand through his sweaty hair. "I should go."

"It's late. You can stay, or at least take a shower. We have lots of spare bedrooms," she said, taking another sip of water.

"I'm going to head out. But I'll see you in the morning," he said. He scooped Arlena up inside one of his large biceps and kissed her passionately on the mouth. Penelope looked away, but she didn't think either of them cared she was standing there. Penelope retrieved the wine key from the floor and opened the bottle on the island.

Finally coming up for air, Sam said, "Penelope...Wife of Odysseus." He set Arlena gently back on the ground and turned to Penelope. "I'm reading a script about them. It's pretty intense, maybe too intense even for me. By the way, you make amazing crab dip." With that he grabbed his heavy leather jacket from the row of hooks by the door and draped it over his shoulders. He kissed Arlena again, this time tenderly on the top of her head, and then headed out the door backwards, bowing deeply to the two of them as he left.

Arlena closed the door behind him and turned to face Penelope, leaning on the door. The two friends looked at each other, listening to Sam's Hummer roar down the driveway. When the engine had faded away, Arlena grabbed a wine glass for herself, motioning for Penelope to fill it.

Penelope poured. "So, what happened?"

"He's very interesting." Arlena took a big sip of wine. She was jumpy and preoccupied, mentally cataloging the highlights of her evening with Sam Cavanaugh.

"Did you guys...?" Penelope said, taking her own sip of wine, eyeing Arlena mischievously.

"No. You know I don't play things that way." Arlena drummed her polished nails lightly on her glass.

"I'm glad you had fun," Penelope said. She paused a beat before continuing. "I talked to Detective Baglioni at the hospital after you guys left. It doesn't sound like they've gotten much farther on the case."

Arlena's blissful mood dipped. "You think he would've figured out what happened to Holly by now."

Penelope thought for a minute then went to her messenger bag and pulled out her iPad. "Maybe they have and they can't say." She sat down on a stool and swiped the tablet to life. She opened her search engine and typed "Holly Anderson, New Jersey." Within seconds the screen was filled with links to websites and a row of images of different girls, all presumably named Holly Anderson.

Arlena looked over her shoulder at the screen. "There are lots of Holly Andersons, looks like. Click on the *Ledger* article again, see if it's been updated."

Penelope opened up the website and scrolled through the piece. "Look, breaking news at the top. It says she was a high school student from New York, and that her death has been ruled a homicide by investigators."

Arlena put her glass down on the island and looked closer at the screen.

Penelope brushed the screen with her finger. "That's her," she said, pointing to a picture halfway down the article. It was a school picture of Holly, smiling thinly in front of a mottled blue backdrop.

"Pretty girl, so young," Arlena said.

Penelope looked at the girl's deep brown eyes and a wave of sadness washed over her. She placed the iPad down on the counter and took a breath, fighting a rush of unexpected tears.

Arlena rubbed her shoulders. "Hey, it's going to be all right," she said softly.

"I'm sorry. But how could someone murder a girl who isn't even out of high school? What could she have possibly done to deserve that?"

Arlena shook her head and rubbed harder. "It's been a long day and it's late. Let's get some rest."

Penelope nodded and tapped the power button on her tablet, darkening the screen.

Penelope was in the middle of a dream. For some reason Sam Cavanaugh was questioning her about her crab dip, dressed as a policeman. A loud crash jerked her awake and she sat straight up in bed. She held her breath, listening intently for more noises. She heard rustling and footsteps downstairs and decided it was coming from the kitchen.

"What the hell?" she whispered, slipping quietly out of bed. She was wearing pink and green plaid pajama bottoms and a tight pink t-shirt with green stars on it. Her stomach did a flip when she remembered she hadn't set the security alarm before heading up to bed. She pictured the scene from earlier, Arlena waving goodbye to Sam at the kitchen door with the disabled alarm pad next to it, the word DISENGAGED on the touch screen. She wondered if Arlena had remembered to arm the system before she'd gone to bed.

Maybe Arlena was sleepwalking. Or maybe Sam was back to do some more workouts with Arlena. A crash from a pan landing on the kitchen floor sent goose bumps down her arms. She knew Arlena wouldn't be cooking anything at one in the morning. She had a rule about not eating anything after eight o'clock. What was Zazoo doing? Normally he'd be barking his head off. Arlena must have him locked up in her room on the other side of the house.

Penelope went out into the hallway and crept down the staircase.

She peered around the corner into the hallway and saw a shadow move across the kitchen floor. There was definitely a man moving around in there. Maybe Sam had decided to come back and spend the night after all.

She heard the flick of a lighter and then smelled cigarette smoke. Nope, it definitely was not Sam, Mr. My-Body-is-a-Temple. No way would he be smoking, especially not in front of Arlena, who hated cigarettes more than she hated cellulite.

Penelope tiptoed on her bare feet to the hall closet and opened it, looking for something to protect herself with. The closet was full of designer coats. Not much protection there. She looked up at the shelf over the coasts and saw the rim of a tennis racket sticking out.

"Better than nothing," she murmured. She grasped the racket in both hands and headed back towards the kitchen, wrinkling her nose at the cigarette smoke. She felt for her cell phone in her back pocket, then remembered she was wearing pajamas and her phone was charging up next to Arlena's phone and iPad on the kitchen counter.

Wonderful place for it to be right now. There was no landline in the house. Neither she nor Arlena were home often enough to justify having a house phone. Arlena could be gone for weeks at a time depending on her filming schedule.

She came to the left-hand doorway of the kitchen and peeked inside. A taller than average man was standing in front of the open refrigerator, eyeing the contents, as if contemplating making a sandwich. He wore a knit hat and a bulky plaid coat with a turned-up collar that hid his face from her view, faded skinny jeans and big black work boots. A path of melted snow trailed behind him from the kitchen door. A cigarette dangled between two of the fingers that were propped on top of the refrigerator door.

Zazoo sat on his bed, eyeing the man at the refrigerator and chewing greedily on a turkey hot dog that clearly had been used to buy his silence.

Traitor. Penelope rolled her eyes at their faithful watchdog.

Just then Penelope saw Arlena from the opposite doorway

to the kitchen. She was looking at the man from behind also, sleepy fury etched on her face. She held a large red rubber band in her hands, one of the resistance bands from the workout room. Arlena used the bands to tone and tighten but right now she was wielding it like a garrote. Penelope wasn't sure if it was the intruder or the fact that he was smoking in her house, but she had never seen Arlena so angry.

The man, making his snack choice, grabbed a container of leftover turkey chili and a beer from the refrigerator. Still out of sight, Penelope motioned to Arlena, who finally realized she had been lurking in the opposite doorway.

Arlena nodded at Penelope and started doing those hand and finger motions that Penelope saw actors do on cop shows, the ones that she could never figure out the meaning of. Arlena pointed two fingers at her own eyes and then pointed them at Penelope then made a circle with her index finger pointing towards the floor. Penelope nodded. She assumed she was supposed to join Arlena in an ambush. Or maybe Arlena was telling her she had mascara smeared under her eyes. Either way, Arlena began counting silently with her fingers, one, two...

On three they rushed into the kitchen. Penelope smashed the tennis racket down on top of the man's head and Arlena jumped up, attempting to lasso him with her exercise band. It must have been her first time trying this particular move, because she only managed to snag the hat off of his head and pull his hair.

"Ouch! What the hell?" he said, spinning around, his hat falling to the floor.

"Max," Arlena yelled. "You little shit! You scared the hell out of us. And why are you smoking in here?"

"I thought you were out of town. What are you doing here?"

"I live here. Unlike you." She pointed to the sink and Max Madison, Arlena's half-brother, went over and ran his cigarette under a stream of water. He threw it into the trash can under the sink.

"I know you live here. Aren't you filming?"

Penelope dropped the tennis racket to the floor. "I'm going back to bed."

"Max, apologize to Penelope," Arlena shouted.

"Sorry, Pen." Max flashed his perfectly shaped dimples. He was tall and dark like Arlena, but had sharp blue eyes with long black lashes. He was outrageously handsome and he knew it. The Madisons had clearly won the genetic lottery.

Penelope sighed and headed back upstairs. "I'll sleep when I'm dead."

CHAPTER 7

Penelope was so exhausted when the alarm went off a few hours later that she didn't believe it could possibly be the next morning. She stumbled into the bathroom and turned her shower on, nudging the knob to make the water as hot as she could stand. She stood under the stream for an extra five minutes, laying out the upcoming day in her mind, making mental notes and lists of things to do when she got to work. By the time she dried off, swiped some mascara onto her lashes and glossed her lips, she began to feel human again. She pulled on a pair of skinny jeans and a camel-colored knit sweater and headed downstairs, not quite bouncing down the steps but not dragging either.

She slipped out of the kitchen door, remembering to arm the security system before she left. Zazoo must have gone into Arlena's room to sleep. His bed was empty except for a stuffed hot dog chew toy.

She had no idea where Max ended up. He usually crashed in one of the spare rooms upstairs when he was in town. He was one of those people who always left everything a shade out of order behind him, but he was a nice guy and a good brother to Arlena.

Arlena and Max hadn't grown up together and had only become close as adults. Their father was screen legend Randall Madison who had been acting in movies since before they were born. Randall had been married and divorced numerous times, and Max and Arlena were just two of his many children. Arlena still hadn't met several of her half-siblings. She told Penelope that whenever her dad began filming a new movie, he'd find a new love of his life. Randall Madison had been married to Arlena's mother for a brief time, but not long enough for Arlena to remember living with him. Max was the result of a fling Randall had a several years later with a set designer in Tucson.

Penelope's phone buzzed in her back pocket. She pulled it up to her ear as she looked over the produce invoices lying in front of her on the steel countertop in the kitchen truck.

"Hello?"

"Hi, Penelope, it's Detective Baglioni." His voice was warm and smooth. A tingly finger drew a line down Penelope's spine and she stood up straight.

"Joey...hi," Penelope said. She turned to lean against the counter and ran a hand through her long blond hair.

"I hope I'm not catching you at a bad time. I'd like to meet with you sometime today. With Miss Madison also. I'd like to ask you both a few more questions concerning the case."

"Um, sure. We're on set in downtown South Point. Lunch break is at one, so we could talk after I get everything set up. Arlena should have a minute then too. I'm in the big white tent. You can have lunch with us if you'd like." Penelope figured she was the only person in the world who was looking forward to a police officer coming to question her.

"That's nice of you. I'll see you around one."

Penelope ended the call and then looked down at her

clothes. Luckily her black kitchen apron wasn't totally smeared with food and her clothes were pretty clean. She decided to head over to the makeup trailer before lunch to see if Kelley could touch her up before Joey arrived. Couldn't hurt.

CHAPTER 8

Detective Baglioni pushed himself away from the table and wiped his mouth.

"Very good. Excellent."

"Thank you. But you only had a salad and some roasted chicken. Can I get you anything else?" Penelope sat across from him at one of the long dining tables under the tent. Many of the cast and crew had already eaten lunch and the tables were mostly empty, only a few of the extras and crew members lingered. Penelope's staff was consolidating the leftover food and breaking down the steam trays on the service station behind them.

"No, that's plenty for me."

"You said on the phone you had more questions about the case?"

"Yes," Joey said, crumpling his napkin in his fist. He glanced around to see if anyone was within earshot of them, but the remaining diners were farther away, talking with each other or reading script pages. He pulled a small manila envelope out of his coat pocket and handed it to Penelope.

She glanced at him and bent back the metal clasps, lifting up the flap. Inside were several pictures of a beautiful young girl with dark hair and olive skin. Penelope recognized her right away as Holly Anderson.

"These look like headshots," Penelope said. She placed them down one by one on the table. There were six different poses of her in the photos. Some were just of her face, her head tilted slightly and smiling or looking straight at the camera with a sultry glance. Then there was a bathing suit shot and a shot of her in tight workout shorts and a tank top, looking like a fitness model. In another picture she was dressed like an action heroine or a video game character. She looked beautiful and confident in each picture.

"Holly was an aspiring actress," Joey said. "She was trying to break into the industry, going on auditions and sending these out."

"Wow. She was pretty," Penelope said, feeling the familiar sadness pressing on her chest. "What was she doing on our street that night?"

"That's what I came to ask you. We found your address on a piece of paper in her pocket. She must have been on her way to see you."

"Me? Why?"

"Maybe not you. Maybe she was trying to get Arlena's attention, hoping to meet her to further her career ambitions."

"But knocking on our door in the middle of the night during a blizzard?"

"I agree the timing doesn't make sense. Where is Arlena? I didn't see her sitting with the rest of the diners."

"Oh, she usually does. She likes to eat with everyone. But she and Sam asked to take lunch in her trailer so they could run some lines before their scene this afternoon."

"Run lines. Is that what the kids are calling it these days? They looked pretty cozy yesterday at the hospital."

Penelope blushed and picked up her phone to text Arlena,

giving her a warning they were heading her way. "That's what she said they were doing. I guess we'll have to go see for ourselves."

"I guess we will," Joey said, suppressing a smile.

Penelope thought about what it would be like to run some lines of her own with Joey. Then her pink cheeks turned a deep red and she quickly hopped up from the table. "Let's go," she said, busying herself with clearing their lunch trays.

CHAPTER 9

They heard the yelling from Arlena's trailer before they got there.

"You bastard! You know how much this means to me," Arlena shouted.

"But you don't know what you want...or what being with you means to me," Sam yelled back.

Joey stopped abruptly and glanced at Penelope, a look of warning on his face. He stepped in front of her, putting his hand on her forearm to stop her. Her skin tingled under his touch. She nudged him with her shoulder and giggled.

"What's funny? Sounds like a domestic happening in there," Joey said. "Those two having problems with each other?"

"They're running lines. They're a troubled married couple in this movie, remember?"

The yelling stopped and they climbed the little metal staircase to the trailer door. Joey glanced at Penelope and knocked on the door. "Hello? Miss Madison? It's Detective Baglioni. I'm with Penelope."

They heard faint male and female mumbling and then a rustling from behind the door.

"Just a minute..."

Penelope looked away, avoiding eye contact with Joey. A few seconds later the door flew open and Arlena stood there, smiling, flushed and beautiful in a tank top and yoga pants, her feet bare.

"Come in," she said in the sexy version of her voice.

"Thank you. Sorry to intrude," Joey said, glancing around the trailer. "I know you're working but we have some new information about the murdered girl. Hello again, Mr. Cavanaugh," Joey said, nodding to Sam. He was sitting in the middle of Arlena's white leather couch, his arms stretched open behind him, spanning the entire back of it.

"Detective," he said. Sam was shirtless and wore tight jeans that rode low on his hips, leaving little to the imagination. He had what they called six-pack abs, but they looked more like a ten or twelve pack. The man didn't have an ounce of fat on him. Anywhere. And he looked tan, but not too tan, in the middle of New Jersey winter. His blond hair was spiked, like he'd just rolled out of bed, though it probably took a while to make it look like that. Kelley must've taken her time to get the artfully tossed, bed-head look for him.

"I'll get going so you guys can talk," Sam said.

"No, please stay. Anything the police have to say to me they can say in front of you," Arlena said.

Penelope wondered again if Sam and Arlena realized they were not in fact legally married to each other. Arlena perched on the arm of the sofa next to Sam, placing her perfectly shaped feet on his muscular thigh.

"As long as it's okay with you, it's fine with me," Joey said. He took the manila envelope he had shown to Penelope and handed it to Arlena. "Look at these photos. We think Holly Anderson was attempting to contact you on the night she was killed."

"For what reason?" Arlena pulled out the stack of photos and began looking through them.

"That's what we're trying to determine. We also found the

car service she used to get out to your place. Livery cab left her on your street per her instructions."

"And the driver left her outside on a freezing night?"

"Seems that way. She told him she lived at your house and that she was your sister."

Arlena looked up from the photos on her lap and stared at Joey. "Sister?"

"That's what she said," Joey said. Penelope sat down in one of the white leather chairs opposite the couch.

"Detective, it's no secret that my father has many children, but to my knowledge they've all been acknowledged and accounted for."

"I've been reading up on your dad," Joey said, nodding.

Arlena sighed, shaking her head. "My father can be careless in his relationships. But he is also very loving and talented." Arlena often sounded resigned when she spoke about her father. Penelope knew he was a source of both amazement and embarrassment for her.

"Anything is possible when it comes to Daddy," she said, shrugging. "I can't say I'd be shocked if it turns out we were related."

Sam laid his hand lightly on Arlena's thigh, gently massaging it. She looked back down at the photos, taking care to study each one before moving on to the next. "She was beautiful."

The last photo in the stack was the one of her in the superhero outfit, Holly in tight leather shorts and a skimpy tank top. Her long black hair hung in two braids down her back, and her hips were cocked, her thin hand perched on one of them. She had a sexy, slightly threatening look on her face.

"Wait a minute. This is my picture," Arlena said.

"Your picture? What do you mean?" Joey said.

"My picture. The same exact outfit and pose. Wait, look

here." Arlena grabbed her iPad off of the glass coffee table in front of her. She opened a folder and scrolled through several thumbnail images until she came to the one she was looking for. It was Arlena in the exact same outfit and pose as Holly's photo. "Look." She handed the iPad to Joey.

"I can see they're very similar."

"Similar? It's an exact copy. I had that taken when I was up for *Soldier of Fortune*. I didn't get the part, but I was in the running."

Joey nodded. "Where was this taken?"

"The photographer's name is Richard Tangelo. He's in the city. He's done lots of shots for me." Arlena leaned back on the couch.

"Are these published anywhere?"

Arlena thought for a moment and said, "I don't think so. I have copies and Richard does, and my agent. They get sent out to directors and casting agents all the time, so I guess they could end up anywhere." She stared at a photo of Holly's face. "She has Daddy's eyes. She looks like us, doesn't she?" She handed the picture to Sam, who nodded.

"Unfortunately, Miss Madison, we have to consider the possibility that Holly Anderson wasn't the target. That maybe she was in the wrong place at the wrong time. And that someone killed her, thinking they were killing you."

"Kill me? What are you talking about?"

Penelope sat up straighter in her chair and Sam's hand stopped moving on Arlena's shoulder.

"We have to consider every aspect of this. This girl thinks that maybe she's your sister. She finds out where you live and comes to your home, all the way from the city, to talk to you about it. She clearly had ambitions to become an actress, like you. If you were being stalked or someone wanted to hurt you, and they saw Holly, someone very physically similar to you on a dark street outside of your home. They may have killed her by mistake."

"Do you have any evidence of anything like that happening or are you guessing?" Arlena asked.

"Right now that's just one possible scenario. You have to admit you're very much in the public eye and have been for years. Unfortunately, being a celebrity brings with it a certain level of negative attention sometimes from some very unstable people. It's not uncommon for fans to become fixated." He shrugged, his suit jacket lifting a bit each time he made a point. "And it's a bit too coincidental in my opinion that a girl who resembles you gets murdered right outside your property. Add to that your run-in with the golf cart yesterday...I'm not saying you're definitely the target of a killer, but we have to think seriously about your safety in case you are."

"Did you say you talked to the cab driver?" Penelope asked.

"He says he dropped her off outside your neighbor's gate, then he left to pick up another fare. We searched the car but nothing turned up. His next passenger confirmed the timing. Holly lived on the Lower East Side with her parents and two younger brothers. Good girl, good grades. They'd been letting her audition for plays and commercials, supporting her acting ambitions."

"Parents, as in mother and father? How did she come to think she was Arlena's sister?" Penelope asked.

"We're still working on that. She was sixteen and her room was filled with the usual, posters, school collages and pictures. But she had obviously done some research on you and your family." He nodded at Arlena. "We found hundreds of searches in her computer history for Arlena and Randall Madison, your other siblings and your dad's various girlfriends. Maybe she was trying to find a link between you and herself or prove something about her past, real or imagined."

"Who would want to kill me?" Arlena asked quietly.

"Think about it. Have you noticed anything out of the ordinary? Anyone acting strangely?"

Arlena pondered his question for a moment, then shook her head. "Nothing stands out. I've been so busy getting ready for this movie I haven't been out much at all. Just home rehearsing, and my usual routine."

"Are you sure? No unusual contact from anyone? It doesn't have to be negative in nature, maybe someone trying to get in touch with you to figure out your routine?" Joey urged.

"You mean like a potential stalker?" Arlena asked, shaking her head. "That would be a nightmare. The only stalker I've had any contact with wasn't stalking me, she was stalking Vance." She cut her eyes sideways at Sam to judge his reaction, who didn't seem to have any. He continued to draw light circles with his hand on Arlena's back.

"Your ex-boyfriend, Vance Reynolds?"

Arlena nodded. "She was arrested once for climbing over the wall of our house in LA. She ran halfway across the lawn before one of Vance's security guards tackled her. We weren't even at the house that week. We were off on the boat together." Again she glanced guiltily at Sam but he had no reaction. Apparently he wasn't the jealous type.

"Her name is Jocelyn Honeywell." Arlena swiped the iPad in her lap to life again and tapped on Google, searching for images of Vance's stalker.

When she handed the iPad to Joey, Penelope saw that over a hundred and fifty images had come up. Most of them were of Vance and Arlena, probably because they had been tagged in the photos.

"Have you had any contact with Jocelyn since her arrest?" Joey asked, swiping through the images.

"None. She probably lost any interest she might have had in

me after we split. When we broke up that cleared the way for her to be with him." Arlena smirked. "So why would she come after me?"

"You can't know what's going on in someone's mind. It's worth checking out," Joey said.

"We're going to have to get to our location soon, Detective," Sam said, glancing at his Rolex.

"All right. I appreciate your time. All of you," he said, looking at Penelope. "I'll keep you updated about any progress. In the meantime, please be careful, Miss Madison. Don't take any unnecessary chances. And if anyone or anything seems off or you feel threatened, get in touch with us right away." He stood up and reached out a hand to Arlena, which she gently shook. "Mr. Cavanaugh." He nodded at Sam.

"Call me Sam."

"Until next time," Joey said. "Would you mind walking me out, Penny?"

"Sure," she said.

"Thank you for lunch," Joey said as they walked back through the production lot.

"My pleasure. Thanks for filling us in on Holly. I hope you find out who did this soon."

They passed the catering tent and stopped at Joey's black sedan in the parking area. Joey took a step closer to Penelope and adjusted his jacket. Penelope shivered in the cold air.

"You have my number, right?"

"I have your card."

"Do me a favor and put my number in your phone. That way you can call me if anything comes to mind or if you remember anything else that might be helpful."

"Okay, I'll do that."

"Or you can call if you have any questions about anything...about the case."

Penelope felt like if she said anything else she might begin to ramble. She looked up into his eyes, then looked away quickly, shifting from foot to foot as she shivered in the cold. A smile touched the corners of his mouth.

He bent his head down towards hers and her heart skipped once. She tilted her head slightly, anticipating the brush of his lips, but instead he leaned down and whispered in her ear. "That roasted chicken was amazing. Thank you." His lips fluttered over her ear and his stubbly cheek brushed lightly against her smooth one as he stood back up. He took a step back towards the car.

Penelope exhaled. "You're welcome. Thanks for stopping by."

"I'll be in touch, Penny Blue," he said, opening the car door and sliding behind the wheel.

Penelope sat up front in the cab of the kitchen truck which she had fashioned into a mini office. She was trying to forget how good Joey looked and the almost-kiss by focusing on payroll and order sheets. It wasn't working, but she plowed ahead anyway.

Francis knocked on the glass window. She rolled it down, letting in the bitter air.

"Hey, Francis. What's up?"

"I wanted to double check on tomorrow's menu. Italian, right?"

"As requested by Sal. You take lead and make your homemade sauce. Get it started tonight before we wrap so it has time to get really tasty overnight."

"You got it, Boss. *Viva Italiano!*" He swaggered away, his baggy chef pants and coat draped over his tall frame. Francis was the first chef Penelope had hired for Red Carpet Catering. They'd worked together on a commercial a few years earlier when they were both starting out. He was only nineteen years old then and had amazing energy, always pitching in wherever the crew needed help. And luckily he had the culinary chops too. His food was inspired. Francis was known to go home and bake Italian desserts after a long day of cooking on set and bring them in the next day for the kitchen crew to try. When Penelope asked him to join her crew, he stood up in the little coffee shop they were meeting in and hugged her, lifting her out of her chair.

They'd built the rest of their team thoughtfully through recommendations or previous work contacts. Penelope knew she had a solid team and Francis as her Sous was her right-hand.

The walkie-talkie chirped on the dashboard. "That's it for today. Everybody go home," said Sal in his New Jersey growl.

Penelope was so glad they were finished for the day and it was still light outside. She just wanted to go home, enjoy a warm bowl of soup and get into bed. If she was lucky, she might actually get a decent amount of sleep tonight.

CHAPTER 10

Penelope woke to warm sunlight and the sound of pots and pans clanking downstairs. She knew Arlena wouldn't be cooking anything. It took her sleepy brain a minute to remember that Max was staying with them and was probably making himself some breakfast.

She wandered into the kitchen, yawning and running her hands through her hair. She woke for the first time that week with the refreshed feeling that comes after a night of peaceful, uninterrupted sleep.

A bunch of pans sat on top of the stove's gas burners, blue flames flickering under them. Something in the oven smelled wonderful. Zazoo was perched happily on his bed, chewing on a slender rawhide straw. Max heard Penelope come in and he spun around.

"Hey, Penelope. Lovely day."

Lovely Day was a movie that Penelope had worked on and she was wearing the film's t-shirt the first time she'd met Max, so he always greeted her that way for some reason. It was kind of nice, she supposed.

"Hey, Max," she said, sliding onto one of the stools in front of the black marble kitchen island.

"Coffee?" He grabbed the carafe from the coffeemaker and a large mug, making his way over to her from the stove.

Penelope nodded and he poured her a cup, then grabbed a container of half and half from the refrigerator and handed it to her. Penelope mixed her coffee to her liking and took a sip. "What are you up to over there?" she asked, looking over his shoulder at the stove.

"Croissants in the oven and crepes on the stove. Arlena texted me last night and said you guys had an afternoon call today so I thought I'd treat you to a nice breakfast to make up for scaring the crap out of you the other night."

"Breakfast should totally make up for that. Sorry for smashing you with a tennis racket."

Max leaned on the island and gazed at her. He was wearing pajama bottoms and a dark blue t-shirt stretched tightly across his lean torso.

"What kind of crepes are you making?"

"Whatever you desire," he said. His dimples were out again and his black hair was mussed in a sexy, not so random way.

"I desire...you know what? Surprise me."

"As you wish." He turned back to the stove.

Penelope sipped her coffee and admired Max's muscular back as he chopped and whisked.

"Arlena told me about you finding that poor girl out in the street. How are you holding up?" Max asked without turning around.

"I'm okay," Penelope said. "I keep thinking about her, though."

"And they don't know who did it?" he asked, tilting the pan from side to side to create a thin layer of batter.

"Not yet. They're still looking into everything," Penelope said, eyeing his technique. "They think there might be a connection to Arlena with the accident on the set."

Max's shoulders tensed and he turned around. "What do you mean? Someone might be trying to kill my sister?"

Penelope sat up straighter, worried she'd said too much. "No, they just want her to be careful, in case the two things are related."

Max relaxed slightly and said, "If it's not a coincidence, maybe Arlena should hire some security."

"I think Sam Cavanaugh is volunteering for the job," Penelope said.

"Really?" Max asked, turning back to the stove.

Once again, Penelope was afraid she'd overstepped. She didn't want Arlena to think she'd been talking about her behind her back to Max. She quickly changed the subject. "Who taught you how to make crepes?"

"Dear old Dad." Max chuckled. "Well, not really. He got me a job on the catering crew on *Rolling Thunder* back in Tucson. I was fifteen and they hired me to help serve and wash dishes. The head chef liked me, and he taught me a few things. By the end of the shoot I was doing more cooking than dishwashing."

Rolling Thunder was a motorcycle movie Randall had starred in, which had later become a cult classic. Penelope and Arlena had watched it together in the den with a big bowl of popcorn and a bottle of wine. Arlena had all of her dad's movies on DVD, and every so often she got in the mood to watch them when she hadn't seen him in a while.

"That was a fun shoot," he continued. "It was a cool summer job and I got to spend time with Dad. He also spent a lot of time with the head makeup artist on that one." Max winked at her. "But we had some good times. He taught me how to ride a motorcycle too."

"It's never a bad thing to know how to cook," Penelope said.

"It does help with charming the ladies," he said, shrugging. Penelope wondered what it would be like to date Max. She supposed if he was like his father his relationships were probably exciting and brief.

"So what are you up to these days?" Penelope asked.

"My agent is sending me up for a few movies," Max said, refilling her coffee cup. "Nothing solid yet, I've been going on some auditions, unfortunately no leading roles. I shot a pilot for MTV that looks promising."

"Oh yeah? What's it about?"

"It's a reality show about celebrity's kids. We all live together in an apartment in the city, go on auditions, fight with each other, fight with our parents. You know, the usual. The scripts look good so I'm hoping it comes through." He gently folded over the crepe and slid it onto a plate. He garnished it with a sliced a strawberry.

"What did you mean by scripts? Isn't it a reality show?"

"Reality," Max chuckled. "The show has a team of writers. So it's a version of reality, I guess. They make us sound better. But it's based on what we would actually say." Max opened the oven and plucked out three croissants, placing them on a platter on the island counter.

Penelope eyed Max's work. "Hey, if the pilot doesn't work out, you can come and work for me."

"That might be too tempting, Pen. I wouldn't be able to concentrate on my work with you around all the time, cooking together in a warm, close kitchen with all that heat." Max raised his eyebrows suggestively, taking a sip of his coffee. He leaned on the counter, watching her eat.

Penny rolled her eyes. "Yeah, right. I think you could probably handle it." Arlena had told Penelope that Max had a crush on her. But Penelope knew Max was naturally flirtatious with everyone. He was a sweet young guy but also an unapologetic Lothario. Penelope was flattered by the attention but didn't kid herself. She knew Max spread his attention around generously with lots of girls, both serious prospects and passing flirtations. She figured she was getting a taste of what lots of women through the decades had experienced from Randall Madison as well...the apple not falling far from the tree theory.

"I'll keep a culinary career in mind as my safety if the whole leading man thing doesn't work out."

Arlena came wandering into the kitchen in a short silk pajama set and high heeled fuzzy slippers. Zazoo's ears perked up and he let out a yip, then went back to chewing on his rawhide.

"Hey, sis. Breakfast?" Max said. He went over and picked her up in a hug. "Pen told me we have to watch out for you, that things might be getting dangerous." He set her down and put his hands on her shoulders. "Whatever you need."

"Thanks, Max," Arlena said gratefully. She glanced at Penny's almost finished crepe. "I'll have egg whites. Maybe some veggies. I've got a lingerie scene today, can't look bloated." Arlena slid onto the stool next to Penelope and Max placed a cup of coffee in front of her.

"Where have you been staying, Max?" Penelope asked, finishing the last bite of crepe and ripping off a piece of croissant.

Arlena glanced longingly at the flaky pastry then looked back down into her black coffee. After taking a bite, Penelope discretely placed the pastry out of sight on the far side of her plate.

"I've been crashing here and there. I was staying with a girl on the Upper West Side, but that's ended so I'm a free agent. If the pilot comes through I'll be living in the West Village in the building the network leased for the show. The apartment looks like the *Friends* set." He winked at Penelope. She glanced away and took another sip of coffee.

"Where will you live if the pilot doesn't come through? Maybe it's time you get your own apartment," Arlena said.

Max turned back to the stove. "With my luck I'll sign a lease, and the next day get hired onto a movie and be gone six months. Who knows, maybe I'll end up in LA. I'll travel light and go where the next job is. I can always crash with Dad if a part doesn't come through right away. I'm not too worried about it."

CHAPTER 11

They had an afternoon call which meant the crew would be filming into the night. Penelope and her team would be putting on lunch and dinner and after they wrapped it would be their weekend. Penelope was excited to have her Italian feast for the crew and then have a nice rest afterwards to recover from a long week.

Francis had arrived before her and was stirring a big pot of sauce on the stove. The air inside the kitchen truck was perfumed with the smell of ripe tomatoes and basil.

"Good morning, Francis," Penelope said as she looked into the pot at the deep red sauce. "That smells so good. Thanks for making it."

"No problem. It's Grandma Ricci's recipe. We're not supposed to talk about it in the family, but we always like Grandma Ricci's sauce better than Grandma Bianchi's sauce. But we make both, every other weekend. Mama switches it up for Sunday dinner to keep peace in the family."

"You'll have to make me the Bianchi version next time. I'll be an unbiased judge, like in a competition." She patted him on the shoulder.

"Yeah, right. What do you know about marinara sauce?" he teased.

"Irish people eat Italian all the time," she said, slapping him lightly on the back.

"Whatever you say, Boss. So this sauce goes into the lasagna, stuffed shells and the seafood ragout. What else are we doing?"

"Let's do some bruschetta and flatbread pizzas, cut into individual pieces for the starters. Get one of the guys to make basil pesto and some tapenade. Let's give them a nice variety. We'll use whatever looks freshest today."

Francis nodded his agreement. He was still watching and stirring his sauce over the big steel rim of the pot.

"Remember, keep the shellfish for the ragout contained to one cutting board and wash the knives right after. I don't want any cross contamination. We have a few allergies on set. Definitely keep it away from Arlena."

"Right. No problem, Boss."

"Good job, Penelope," Sal said, wiping a smear of red sauce from the corner of his mouth. "Delicious sauce." He nodded appreciatively from his seat in the dining tent. He sat next to Paige, who had pushed her plate aside and was jotting notes on a copy of a script next to him.

"Thanks, Sal. Francis made it. I'll be sure to let him know you liked it."

"Please do. And those desserts! So good."

Towards the end of Italian feast night, Penelope's crew had laid out some beautiful dessert trays with mini tiramisu, cannoli and a variety of gelatos.

Penelope sat down across from Sal and Paige at the long dining table and swiped a few crumbs from the white table cloth. She drank coffee from a ceramic mug and watched Sal finish scoop the last few crumbs form his plate. "I've been in this business a long time. It's important to treat your people right so you get the best from them in return." Sal picked up another mini cannoli. "Look at them." He spread his arms around the tent at the other diners. "Who wouldn't be happy right now?"

Sal was a handsome older man, compact and muscular. He wore a soft beige cable knit sweater with jeans and expensive leather boots. His smiles were infrequent but Penelope noticed when he ate her food they came more often. Paige was very different from him with her tall lean frame. Penelope eyed her discretely and figured she was probably a lot younger than her husband, maybe by more than twenty years.

"We can do another theme night, give everyone something to look forward to."

"Good idea. I like the way you think, kiddo. All right, the last scene of the week is coming up and then I can send you all home for a couple of days of rest. How's that for boosting morale?" He pulled the walkie-talkie off from his belt and pressed the button. "Fifteen minutes to location, everyone."

"Roger that," someone responded. Sal had initiated the chain reaction that would follow, gathering everyone together to head back into action.

"Sal, remember we were going to go over my notes before the scene," Paige began, holding up a few of her marked up pages.

Sal put an arm around Paige's shoulders and looked down at her work. "I'll look at your notes on the way." He picked up Paige's script and stood up from the table, heading out of the dining tent.

The final scene of the week was a love scene between Sam and Arlena. It took place on a closed set designed to be the couple's bedroom. They were both sitting up in the bed nearly naked, a sheet pulled up to their waists. Arlena, wearing a tiny pink bra, was talking to Kelley as she used a large makeup brush to lightly powder her chest and stomach with bronzer. Although Arlena's skin was nearly flawless, the camera would pick up any imperfections. Kelley's assistant was on the other side of the bed styling Sam's hair, taking tufts of his blond locks and massaging them into different directions.

Sal boomed orders and directions at everyone in the room. Penelope counted fifteen crew members in addition to herself, all working busily around the set. This was a pivotal scene in the movie, which Arlena had started calling "The Naked Scene." Penelope knew she meant more than just physically naked.

Arlena had asked Penelope to sit in on the scene for moral support and she'd agreed, although now that it was happening she felt a bit awkward being there. She straightened the already straight line of soda bottles next to the ice tub.

Arlena looked up at the ceiling so Kelley could apply another layer of mascara to her bottom lashes. When she looked back down, she noticed Penelope standing behind the bank of cameras and smiled gratefully at her. Then she looked down at her barely covered torso and back up at Penelope, shrugging slightly.

Penelope nodded confidently at her and gave her a thumbs up, indicating that Arlena looked beautiful and she could totally pull off this scene, even in a skimpy bra.

Arlena took a deep breath, closing her eyes to create a quiet space in her mind amid the revolving chaos around her. Penelope couldn't imagine how it must feel to have millions of people see you uncovered the way Arlena was now. Penelope felt shy changing out of her running clothes at the gym in front of other people.

Sam looked confident and happy, like it was just another day at the office, joking with the crew members working on his side of the room. Penelope noticed he kept a hand loosely entwined with Arlena's on top of the sheet, squeezing it from time to time. She was still confused about how much of their relationship was real and how much was the roles they were playing. Maybe they really liked each other and their relationship would carry on after Sal wrapped the movie.

"Let's take one and see where we are," Sal said, easing down into his canvas director's chair. He gazed into the center monitor attached to the main camera.

Two other cameras were set up on flanking sides of the scene, pointed at the bed. The one on the left was raised up higher than the other two to provide an aerial angle. The camera on the right was shooting from a perpendicular angle and the main camera shot them level with the bed. Kelley and her assistant were the last to clear the shot, brushing and patting cloths on their faces right up until the last second, then slipping away in opposite directions.

"And...action!" Sal's deep voice rang out. Penelope held her breath and watched.

Arlena rolled on top of Sam, straddling his waist, her lean back and shoulders shimmering under the stage lights. She looked tiny sitting on top of him, her long legs wrapping around him perfectly, her knees resting on the bed at his sides. Her panties matched her bra, thin and pink, leaving little to the imagination. She bent at the waist, hovered over Sam and kissed him. He stroked her hair and pulled her deeper into the kiss.

No one in the room moved or made a sound, the room was perfectly still except for Sam and Arlena. Penelope watched them transform into a married couple and create the illusion of an intimate bedroom encounter, all while surrounded by a crowd. Penelope had never watched Arlena on set before, and at that moment she knew Arlena was an amazing actress by anyone's standards.

Arlena sat back up and said softly, "I love you so much, Preston."

"I love you too," was Sam's response. "You're a perfect wife and I don't want anything to change between us." He sat up in the bed and hugged her fiercely to his chest, crushing her small frame into his.

"We're not going to change, Sam..."

"Cut," Sal yelled. "It's Preston, dear. Not Sam."

Arlena looked over her shoulder at Sal. "Sal, I'm so sorry."

"It's fine, kiddo. Let's take it again from the kiss," Sal said.

The couple retook their positions and began again, Sam laying back down and Arlena bending down to kiss him from her straddling position on his waist.

"You are a perfect wife and I don't want anything to change for us," Sam said. He sat up and hugged her to his chest again.

"We're not going to change, Preston. But a baby, especially a baby who needs a family...that's a positive change that can only make us stronger." Arlena spoke with quiet confidence. She pushed out of the hug and put her hands on either side of his face, looking into his eyes.

"But what if it wrecks us? What if a child ruins everything we've built together?" Sam asked.

"How could that be? We're perfectly happy. We'd only be adding more happiness," Arlena said, kissing him lightly on the lips.

Sam looked away from her and leaned back onto the headboard. "Molly, I'm scared about the future. I don't want all of this to go away."

"It's not, Preston. I promise."

"I slept with someone else," Sam said quietly, not making eye contact with Arlena.

"What are you talking about?" Arlena said. Penelope could see the muscles in her back become rigid.

"When I was in New York the last time," he whispered. His eyes became shiny with tears. Penelope held her breath once again, mesmerized by the scene.

"Preston, what are you saying?"

"I slept with my old girlfriend from high school. I ran into her after my meeting. She was staying at the same hotel. It wasn't planned." He was pleading now. "We were in the bar and ran into each other...it was a mistake. We fell into it."

Arlena drew back from him, her shoulders now wilting as she searched his face.

"Molly, please. It was a mistake," Sam said. "I don't want anything to change."

Arlena drew back her hand and slapped him hard across the face. Penelope's heart did a flip in her chest and a wave of emotion rippled across everyone in the room. Pent up tears fell from Sam's eyes and he once again crushed her to his chest.

Arlena stayed totally still and quiet, sinking into him as he hugged her, not wanting to let go as they rocked together on the bed.

"How can you say that when what you did changes everything about us?" she whispered wetly in his ear.

"And...cut," Sal said quietly from behind the monitor. Quiet applause began from a crew member in the corner of the room and Penelope joined in. She took a deep breath, fighting back tears she couldn't quite understand.

Arlena rolled off of Sam back to her original place on the bed. Penelope could see that she was also crying and Sam was wiping his face of tears.

"Good job, babe," he said to her, leaning in for a kiss.

"You too, Sam." She kissed him back then gave him a big hug. "Sorry about the slap. I got carried away."

"It's all good. It was real, I'll give you that," Sam said, smiling and rubbing the red spot on his cheek.

Kelley and her assistant took their spots on either side of the bed and began reapplying powder, and un-smudging Arlena's lipstick and mascara.

"Let's get some pancake on that cheek," Kelley muttered, eyeing Sam's face.

"All right everyone, we're doing another take," Sal said. "This time, Sam, I want you to be less confident in the beginning. You know you're about to tell your wife that you've been unfaithful, so remember that is looming and work up to the emotion of contrition."

"You got it, Sal," Sam said. Penelope knew confidence wasn't Sam's problem. Showing a lack of confidence would be where his acting abilities came in.

Arlena waved her over and Penelope stepped carefully through the cables that snaked across the floor.

"That was great," Penelope said. Sam was laughing with one of the grips as he adjusted one of the lamps behind the bed.

"You'd tell me, right? I mean, friends tell friends if they look terrible or sound ridiculous."

"Of course, I would tell you. But there's nothing to tell."

"I'm trying to be sexy, mad and sad all at the same time. And I want him to agree to get that baby."

"It's all working. I believe every word you're saying."

"Hey, can you get me some water with lemon?" Arlena asked.

"Sure, be right back."

Sal was talking with the cameraman and woman who were manning the flanking shots. He had a roll of papers in his hand that he motioned with, pointing out different spots in the room. He motioned for the script supervisor to join them, a young girl with skinny jeans, black hipster glasses and long red hair. She quickly leafed through the pages in her hand and Sal glanced over her shoulder, pointing out a passage to the camera woman on the left. She nodded and made a note on her copy of the script.

Penelope made her way over to Arlena with a Solo cup filled with ice water and a lemon wedge.

"Thanks," she said gratefully, taking a big sip. Kelley was brushing powder on Arlena's cleavage again.

"You're welcome," Penelope said. "How many times do you think you're going to have to do the scene?"

"I don't know," she said, and took a big sip of water. "Hopefully not too many more."

"Everyone back to one," Sal said, his voice rising above the murmur in the room. He had his arm draped over the cameraman's shoulders, gazing into his monitor.

"Are you finished with this?" Kelley said, indicating Arlena's cup of water. She was twirling a tube of lip gloss in her long fingers.

Arlena nodded and took the last gulp of water, handing the cup back to Penelope. Kelley patted Arlena's mouth gently with a cloth and then carefully began applying the gloss to Arlena's parted lips.

"Clear the shot, please," Sal boomed, his voice even louder. He had taken his seat back behind the main camera.

Penelope gave her a quick wink and went back to the craft table, tossing Arlena's cup into the trash can against the back wall. She quietly poured herself some water from the dispenser on the table.

"And...action!" Sal said, and the room fell silent.

Arlena and Sam rolled back through their scene. As they ran their lines, Penelope noticed Sam's demeanor was a bit more reserved and Arlena's back was more rigid as she perched up on top of him.

Arlena once again raised her hand up to slap Sam and Penelope's stomach tensed in anticipation. But instead of slapping Sam's face, Arlena's hand flew to her throat and she began gasping for air. Penelope saw Sam's eyes grow wide with concern as Arlena struggled to breathe.

"Arlena, what's the matter?" He sat up and eased her off of him.

Arlena motioned frantically at her throat as she tried to pull air through her swelling windpipe. Sal stood up, knocking over his chair and rushed to Arlena's side.

"What's wrong?" Sal asked in a clear loud voice.

Penelope dropped the cup she was holding on the floor, the water splashing against her legs, and ran to the chair in the back of the room where Arlena had left her clothes and bag.

Arlena gasped loudly and motioned to her throat as members of the crew began rushing around in a panic.

Penelope pulled a bright red case with a sparkly letter A on it from the inside zipper of Arlena's bag. She raced over to the bed, pushing past the camera woman, and handed it to Arlena.

Arlena frantically pulled her EpiPen from inside the case and stabbed herself, the needle piercing her upper thigh. Arlena relaxed almost immediately and her breathing became less labored, returning to normal almost immediately. Tears streamed down her cheeks and she closed her eyes, leaning her head against the headboard.

Sam whispered to her. "Arlena, are you okay? You scared the shit out of everyone."

She nodded weakly with her eyes still closed, focusing on taking deep breaths.

"What the hell was that?" Sal yelled to the room. Arlena winced, but didn't open her eyes.

"She had an allergic reaction," Penelope said.

"Allergic reaction? But she was fine five minutes ago."

"Lemons," Arlena whispered. "Were the lemons in the kitchen with the seafood?"

Penelope's heart sank. "I'll have to check." She looked sheepishly at Sal. "I told my crew to contain the kitchen. I can't imagine they would cut lemons for water with the same knife as prepping seafood."

"My leading lady almost dies and the work tonight is ruined because of lemons?" Sal yelled.

"I'm sorry, Sal," Penelope said. She felt like running away, but knew she had to stay and take responsibility for the mistake.

Sal stared angrily at her as he spoke to the rest of the crew. "Everyone have a nice weekend. We'll re-shoot this scene next week. Get out of here." He slapped his rolled up papers on his thigh and stomped off.

Arlena had stopped crying, but her face was still wet with tears. Her lips had swollen up to twice their normal size, like they always did when she came into contact with shellfish. She laid her head down on Sam's chest and he hugged her as the room filled with sounds of the crew shutting down lights and rolling up cables.

Penelope felt horrible. She stood at the edge of the bed, in disbelief that Arlena had suffered from a mistake for which she was ultimately responsible. She leaned down and said, "Arlena, I am so sorry."

Arlena kept her eyes closed but nodded slightly, waving Penelope away. "It was an accident. Thanks for getting my Pen."

Penelope stood back up, the feeling of helplessness gripping her.

Sam glanced at Penelope over Arlena's head. "I'll take care of her."

The on-set EMT weaved her way around the remaining crew members and walked over to the bed to check on Arlena. Penelope decided to find Francis and figure out how they could have poisoned Arlena.

CHAPTER 12

Penelope hurried back to the kitchen truck. Francis and the rest of her crew were working in the prep tent, wiping down tables and loading the dish racks with dirty plates and glasses. They worked at a steady pace but were relaxed and joked with each other as they listened to the upbeat dance music coming from the large speaker on the roof of the truck.

"Hey, Boss," Francis said when she walked into the tent. "We thought they'd be shooting much later than this. They wrap already?"

"Guys, everyone come here for a second," she said, waving them over. The other three chefs joined Francis and they all listened expectantly, waiting to get their instructions for wrapping the week.

"There was an incident on set. Something happened to Arlena." They all took on concerned looks and shifted on their feet, glancing down or gazing at her. "She had an allergic reaction and had to use her EpiPen to stop it."

"Oh man," Francis said. "She all right?"

"She is now," Penelope said. "But she's shaken up and they had to quit early before they got what they needed."

"Shit," one of them mumbled.

"She's severely allergic to shellfish. And I know of at least three other crew members who have allergies too. I know I made it clear that we couldn't let seafood come into contact with anything else in the kitchen," she said, glancing at all of them. "Who cut lemons today?"

Quentin raised his rag over his head.

"Did you use a clean knife and a clean cutting board?"

"Yes ma'am. I absolutely did. Took them right out of the clean bin and got started. I cut oranges first, then limes and lemons. Then I wiped my board down and did the fruit salad."

"And you cut the fruit out here in the tent, not inside the truck?"

"Yep. Over at that table." He motioned to a folding table near the far end of the tent.

"Good, so we can be fairly confident the contamination didn't happen here." Penelope felt a fraction of weight ease off of her shoulders.

"I guess it's good we didn't mess up," Francis said, "but then how did it happen? Arlena still got poisoned."

The set was clearing down for the weekend, everyone busily wrapping up their departments for a much needed break. Penelope couldn't believe the week she'd had. It started with them finding a dead teenager out in front of their house and ended with Arlena having a major allergic reaction. Not to mention the golf cart incident that sent her to the hospital.

Penelope was sitting in the cab of her kitchen truck, sorting through paperwork and thinking about everything that had happened. The windows of the cab had fogged up against the cold air outside and she enjoyed the small measure of privacy they provided. She was exhausted and at different points felt like crying, screaming or punching something. Instead of letting herself get overwhelmed, she focused on mindless paperwork, which always calmed her down.

Penelope considered Arlena's accident earlier in the week. She had suffered a severe blow to the head, enough to send her to the hospital and then home to rest for the day. And now filming was delayed once again due to an incident with Arlena. Penelope hoped Sal wouldn't become frustrated with her because of all the production delays.

They only had two weeks left to finish the movie. Both Sam and Sal were committed to projects right after this one, so if they didn't finish principal filming on schedule the movie wouldn't get made.

Penelope remembered the scene Arlena had filmed earlier in the evening and how exposed she'd been. Arlena had never been fully nude in a movie but Brett Ralston, the creator and director of the *Slash 'Em* film franchise had insisted on her being topless in the most recent film. Arlena flatly refused and tense negotiations began between Brett and Arlena's agent. Arlena eventually walked, citing creative differences, after Brett dug in and threatened to cut her pay in half if she didn't comply with the nudity clause in her contract. Brett eventually hired a younger actress who resembled Arlena, but she had trouble carrying the film, her acting skills, even the limited ones needed to work on a *Slash 'Em* movie, were not up to par. The movie tanked, winning the Razzie for worst film of the year.

A soft knock on the driver's side window brought Penelope back to the present. She rolled the window down, bracing against the cold night air. Francis stood at the door of the truck shuffling in his work boots against the asphalt.

"We're done, Boss. Everything's put away and locked up. And the dirty dishes have already been sent to the restaurant. You need us for anything else?"

"No, that's it. See you next week."

"Me and the guys are heading to Sidewinders for a few beers. You wanna join us?" Francis asked. Sidewinders was a local sports bar outside of town with lots of televisions and cute waitresses in tight short shorts.

"I don't think so. I'm pretty beat."

"Well if you change your mind, you know where to find us."

"Have fun," Penelope said, starting to roll the window back up. "Oh, hey, Francis, I forgot to tell you, Sal loved your sauce. He was happy with the whole meal, actually."

Francis did a mini-fist pump and turned away, heading into the night.

Penelope rolled the window back up and stared out at the darkness for a minute, her mind still restless. She grabbed her iPhone from the truck's dashboard and swiped it to life. She tapped open her contacts and scrolled down to the J's, locating Joey's name. She stared at the screen, her thumb hovering over the "call" button. She glanced at the time on the top of the screen and saw it was eight thirty. She hesitated a few seconds more before tapping it. Penelope's heart skipped once as she put the phone up to her ear and cleared her throat. She couldn't believe that calling a guy at her age still made her nervous. The phone rang six times and Penelope pulled it away from her ear, about to disconnect the call when suddenly she heard a faint "Detective Baglioni."

She put the phone back up to her ear.

"Hello? Detective Baglioni here." He was slightly out of breath like he had rushed to pick up the phone.

"Joey? Hi, it's Penelope."

"Penelope, hi...is everything all right?"

Penelope closed her eyes, feeling awkward. "Not really. There was another incident with Arlena today."

"What happened?" An edge came into Joey's voice.

"She had an allergic reaction to something on the set. Lemons maybe, but we can't figure out how it could have happened."

"Lemons? Arlena is allergic to lemons?" he asked.

"No, she's severely allergic to seafood. But I gave her some water with a lemon wedge in it and right after that she went into a full anaphylactic episode. Had to use her Pen."

"Where is she now?" Joey asked.

"Sam took her home. They had to wrap early."

"She was working when it happened?"

"They were in the middle of a scene," Penelope said, her cheeks flushing as she recalled the image of Arlena struggling to breathe.

"Hmm..." He exhaled into the phone. "Wait, why are you talking about lemons?"

She sighed. "We thought maybe the lemons were cut with the same knife we used to prep the seafood today. Or they somehow came in contact with the same cutting board. But my guy swears he was nowhere near any of it. He was out in the tent, not in the truck."

"So you're saying there's no way it could have happened by accident?"

"That's how I truly feel. But that doesn't change what happened. She was struggling to breathe and..." Penelope grasped the leather padded steering wheel with her free hand, squeezing it tightly.

"The thing is, if you say it wasn't a mistake on the part of your crew, it must have been intentional." Joey was talking quickly, a note of urgency in his voice.

"I hate to think that, Joey," Penelope said. "This movie is Arlena's big break. She's been working so hard. It would be awful if someone was intentionally trying to hurt her."

"Yeah but think about it. We have two life-threatening incidents in the same week, on top of a murder that might involve Arlena in some way. All of that happening in one week is too much to be a coincidence."

"I think you might be right," Penelope said quietly. She squeezed the steering wheel even tighter.

"That's why you called, isn't it?" Joey asked. "Because you think someone might be trying to hurt Arlena."

"Yes," Penelope said reluctantly, shaking her head. "But, I don't know what to think, Joey."

"Hold on a second," Joey said. Penelope heard him put his hand over the phone to muffle his voice as he spoke to someone else in the room. She tried to make out what he was saying but only caught a few words: tonight, case, later and Arlena. The connection opened back up and she heard him clearly again. "Sorry about that."

"It's okay. I know you're busy working," Penelope said.

"Actually, I'm at home."

"Oh, sorry..." Penelope said, wondering who he was talking to.

"I'm thinking I should look into this latest incident. I also have some new information on Holly Anderson."

"Tonight isn't great. Arlena and Sam are at our house. I spoke with Sam to be sure they were home safe and to make sure Arlena was feeling better. He said she took a Valium and went to bed, that was over an hour ago."

"Are you still at work?" Joey said.

"I'm finishing up a few things. Most everyone is already gone for the weekend," Penelope said. "I should go home."

"Tell you what. Why don't you stop by my apartment? I'm in Bradenton. It's on your way."

Bradenton was in between South Point and their house in Glendale. New Jersey was full of quaint little towns, all with their own village greens, shopping areas and residential neighborhoods.

"Sure," Penelope said. "But I'm not interrupting anything, am I?"

"No, it's nothing," he responded quickly.

Penelope paused for a moment. She was tired but didn't want to go home just yet. Maybe talking to Joey would settle her mind so she could get some rest. She also felt a spark of excitement peeking through her exhaustion at seeing him again. "Text me your address. I'll be there in thirty minutes."

"See you then. Drive safe," Joey said and hung up.

Penelope exhaled as she pulled the phone away from her ear, the little wiggle of excitement still churning at the base of her stomach. She flipped down the visor to look at herself in the little mirror on the back of it. "Ugh!" she said when she saw her smudged mascara and the circles under her eyes that looked like faint bruises. She looked pale, paler than she normally looked in the middle of New Jersey winter. She glanced down at her clothes and sighed. She had pulled off her apron after talking to her crew in the tent and hadn't noticed a big stain of red sauce at the bottom of her sweater. Her jeans also looked dingy after twelve hours of walking around on set and working with food. "I need help," she said out loud in the cab.

She grabbed her messenger bag out from under the seat of the truck and tucked her phone inside one of the front pockets. Penelope kept the cab of the truck locked at all times since it was essentially her office and she always kept her bag stashed under there. Only she and Francis had keys and she trusted him completely. She looked through her bag and saw that she had nothing with her, no cosmetic help at all. Just an old tube of lipstick, a tampon and some loose change.

Penelope flipped off the cab light, opened the door and jumped down from the truck, her bag looped over her shoulder. She locked the door behind her and headed towards the trailers on the far end of the lot.

Arlena's trailer was right next to Kelley's, the two biggest on the set. As Penelope approached she saw Freddie, one of the interns, coming out from between the trailers. "Hey, Freddie, is Kelley still in there?"

"I think so," Freddie said, nodding at her door. He was coiling up the cables that ran power to Arlena's home on the set. "At least she was ten minutes ago." He wore an oversized puffy coat over a black t-shirt, a large neon-green skull stretched over his bird-like torso, and baggy jeans that looked like they were about to slip off his narrow hips every time he bent over to pick up the cable slack. Skull tattoos snaked over his hands, and his dyed black hair stuck out in every direction. He turned his back to her and kicked the wound up cable underneath the trailer.

"Thanks," Penelope said to his back. He waved at her and disappeared into the darkness again.

Penelope rapped firmly on Kelley's door. It opened a crack and she peered out hesitantly, but when she saw it was Penelope she swung the door open wide. "Hey, Pen. Come on in," she said through her painted black lips. "I thought everyone was gone." She scrunched the ends of her short black bob.

Penelope stepped inside, pulling the door closed behind her against the frigid air. "Almost, I need a favor. I'm stopping by a friend's place on the way home and I look, well, I look like this." She swept her hands in a dramatic arc from her hair down to her shoes. "Can you make me look presentable? Or at least not like I got dragged behind a bus on the way to his house?"

Kelley laughed out loud, a rare occurrence for the normally reserved girl. "I think I can help." Kelley spun Penelope around and sat her down in the makeup chair facing a mirror lined with large bulbs.

"Fantastic. I thought I looked bad before but the lighting in here lets you know exactly how bad you really look."

Kelley giggled. "You don't look that bad. You're tired. We all are." She released Penelope's hair from its pony tail. Penelope's hair was wavy and thick and she always thought it was too unruly to let it be loose while she was working. A lot of chefs cut their hair short for that reason, but Penelope always thought her hair was one of her best features and didn't want to chop it off. So she tied it back, sometimes for so long letting it down at the end of the day was a huge relief.

"How's Arlena?" Kelley asked as she worked her fingers through Penelope's hair, massaging her scalp with something that smelled like lavender.

"I think she's better. At least she's home in her own bed resting comfortably. Sam's with her."

"That's a relief. I've never seen anything like what I saw her go through today. It was terrible," Kelley said. She moved around to face Penelope on her left side and tilted her face up to the lights, studying her for a moment. Making some kind of determination, she turned towards her makeup tray on the counter at the base of the mirror. She picked up a small palate of foundation and lightly touched a spot with her pinkie under each of Penelope's eyes.

"Look up," she directed as she smoothed the makeup on. Her fingers felt cool and soothing. "Arlena and Sam seem like they have good chemistry. That scene they shot today was something else."

"They sure do," Penelope said.

Kelley applied a light coating of foundation to Penelope's face and then brushed it with a faint bronzer. She dusted her eyelids with a pale gold sparkly eye shadow and swiped her lashes with black mascara.

"Are you wearing this?" Kelley said, looking down at Penelope's stained sweater and stretched out jeans.

"Not if I can help it," Penelope said.

"Oh thank goodness," Kelley said with true relief. "I have a few things here from wardrobe. Let's find something less..."

"Food stained?" Penelope asked.

"Yes, food stained." Kelley agreed, nodding. She pointed to a rolling clothes rack in the corner where various pieces of clothes were hanging. "These are cute." She grabbed a pair of tight black riding pants and a short cropped red jacket and held them up against her tall frame for Penelope to see.

"They're nice. But I think it would look like I was trying too hard. I need casual. I'm only going to an apartment to talk."

"A man's apartment?" Kelley teased.

Penelope glanced away. "But it's a casual man's apartment. Not the North Jersey Horse Riding Club for cocktails and caviar."

"I can work with that. Let's see...how about these? They're stretchy." She held up a pair of dark blue jeans.

"Those are perfect."

"What are you, a size six?" Kelley eyed her from the waist down.

"I was before Italian feast night."

Kelley rolled her eyes and handed her the jeans. Penelope stripped off her dirty jeans and slid on the new pair, feeling them shrink against her legs. She hoped she'd be able to zip them up. She always felt puffier when she was working long hours. It was hard to stick to a good eating and workout routine, much less get enough sleep, when your work days were fifteen hours long.

She buttoned the jeans and glanced in the mirror, happy to see her stomach was still flat and tight above the low riding waistline. She pulled off her stained sweater and stood in her bra, looking eagerly through the wardrobe rack.

"How about this one?" Kelley held up a thin knit sweater, fuzzy and black with a dramatic low neckline. "Trying too hard still?" She waved the sweater on the hanger.

"Let me try it." Penelope slipped it over her head and down into place. It fit perfectly, snug and tight but not too tight, and the neckline did a nice job of featuring her cleavage, which was almost always covered by a chef coat. She fanned her long blond hair over both of her shoulders, turning from side to side to see every angle. "I like it. Thank you so much, Kelley. I owe you one."

"No you don't. You always bring me dinner when I'm too busy to head down to the tent, which no set caterer has ever done for me before." She motioned for Penelope to sit in the makeup chair again. "Let's be sure we've got everything together." She eyed Penelope's face again and turned once again to her makeup tray, grabbing a tube of lip gloss. "One last finishing touch and you're good to go to your casual man's apartment." Kelley tilted Penelope's face upwards with her cool fingers, then unscrewed the lip gloss and began applying it to her lips.

Penelope glanced at the clock on the wall of the trailer and saw she had fifteen minutes to get to Joey's. She had her coat and bag, so she could leave directly from Kelley's trailer. She considered the route she would take, wondering if it would be faster to take the local roads or hop on the Turnpike. A faint, mildly unpleasant smell fluttered past her nostrils and she tilted her head farther back. She thought for a moment that maybe her sweater had been worn by an actress who had gotten sweaty while filming and it hadn't been washed yet. "Do you smell that?" Penelope asked Kelley, lifting her arm to sniff her armpit. It smelled like a dry cleaner's store, so it wasn't her or the sweater.

"I smell something. Yuck, what is that?" Kelley glanced at the wastepaper basket under the counter. "Maybe my assistant threw her lunch out in here." She picked up the waste basket from underneath the counter but it only contained some used cotton balls and a few tissues smeared with makeup.

"Wait…" Penelope grabbed Kelley's wrist and pulled the lip

gloss applicator down to her nose. "It's this. The lip gloss smells funny."

Kelley lifted the tube up to her nose and sniffed. She made a face. "It's gone off or something. Which is ridiculous...this stuff is forty dollars a tube."

Penelope smelled the applicator again. "It hasn't gone off. It smells like clam juice."

CHAPTER 13

Penelope arrived at Joey's apartment slightly after nine thirty, later than she had promised.

He opened the door with a smile. If he thought it was too late for her to visit, he didn't act like it. "There she is," he said, motioning for her to enter. "I was getting ready to put out an APB on you. Here, let me take your coat."

Penelope slid her messenger bag off of her shoulder and onto the floor, propping it up against her leather boot. She slipped off her puffy coat and handed it to him.

"You look nice," he said. He hung her coat in a small closet in the hallway.

Penelope thanked him, temporarily forgetting the makeover Kelley had given her. She picked her messenger bag back up from the floor and clutched it tightly in both hands. "Sorry I'm late. I have something to show you." She reached inside her bag, pulled out five tubes of lip gloss and held them out for him to see.

"Gee, thanks. Normally people bring wine."

The tension left Penelope's shoulders and she let out a small laugh. "Ha. Good one. No, these are Arlena's, from her on-set makeup kit. I think they've been tampered with. One of these might have caused her allergic reaction today."

Joey's face grew serious as he looked down at the tubes in Penelope's hand. "What are you talking about, Penny?"

"They smell...bad. Fishy. I think someone laced these lip gloss tubes with seafood so they would come in contact with Arlena and trigger an attack. The makeup artist used one of these on Arlena right before it happened."

"Hang on." Joey went down the hall into what Penelope guessed was a bathroom, returning a few seconds later with some tissues. "Put them on the counter." He laid the tissues down and she placed them on top of them. "I'll take these in tomorrow and we can find out if they've been tampered with. You know what it means if they have, right?"

"I know. Not an accident," Penelope said, resigning herself to the possibility that someone might be trying to harm her friend.

"Thanks for bringing them to me. I'll check into them first thing in the morning. Let's talk in here." Joey nodded towards the living room. His apartment had an open floor plan anchored by a sleek kitchen with a large island topped with white marble and lined with black swiveling stools. His apartment had a masculine feel, with lots of dark leather and green-tinted glass tables. Joey's walls were lined with framed prints from the Museum of Modern Art.

"Sure, thanks." Penelope wandered into the room, glancing at each of the prints that hung in shiny black frames. "You're an art fan?"

The rear wall of the apartment had a set of double doors leading onto a balcony that stretched the length of the apartment with a view of the Hudson River and the faint lights of the New York City skyline beyond it.

"I can't draw a straight line, but I like to look at things by people who can. I go to shows at the Met from time to time, a gallery show once in a while. Would you like a glass of wine?"

Penelope had been floating slightly outside of herself ever since she discovered the tainted lip gloss, turning the information over and over in her head and thinking about how she would present it to Joey. She didn't remember the drive over to his apartment. But she refocused then, coming back to the present. She was standing in Joey's living room and he was offering her wine.

"Sure...if you're having some," she said.

Joey turned and headed towards the kitchen. He was wearing a tight grey t-shirt and nice fitting dark jeans with soft leather shoes. Penelope realized she hadn't seen him in anything but a suit until now. Well, a suit and an ill-fitting parochial school uniform back in grade school. She glanced around the living room while she waited for him and noticed a bookcase angled next to an overstuffed leather easy chair in the far corner. He had grouped his books by author, and she could see his favorites were Stephen King and Raymond Chandler.

Penelope drifted back towards the kitchen and hoped he didn't think she was too nosy, sizing up his things in the living room. Joey pulled the cork from a bottle of cabernet and poured them each a glass. It almost felt like she was on a date, except for the fact she was here to discuss Holly Anderson's murder.

"What did you want to ask me?" Penelope said, swirling her glass.

Joey came around the island and motioned for them to return to the living room. They sat down next to each other on the couch.

"We've been going through Holly's computer and phone records. She did reach out to Richard Tangelo, Arlena's photographer, to inquire about headshots, but when she asked to make an appointment, he told her how much the consultation alone would cost and she thanked him and said she'd call back, which never happened." Joey took a sip of wine and placed his glass on the table. He picked up a folder lying in the center of the glass. "Tangelo has been working out of his LA office this week, which we were able to confirm with his staff." Joey leafed through a thick stack of documents and reports, finally pulling one from the pile that looked like a phone bill.

Penelope nodded. "It makes sense she would try and get the same headshot photographer if she was trying to follow in Arlena's footsteps. But that doesn't mean anything. Lots of girls want to be like the famous people they admire. And there are tons of photographers in the city."

"That's true. Right now we're looking for connections between Arlena and Holly, tracking Holly's movements." He scanned the list of numbers and pointed to a note he had scrawled next to one of them. "Who is Peter Gessner?" he asked. "Holly called his office multiple times in the two weeks before she was killed."

"That's Arlena's agent," Penelope said, pulling the paper closer to her so they were both holding it by opposite sides of the sheet between them. She slid closer to Joey on the couch, feeling a tingle of static where their legs almost touched. She ignored it and looked through the list.

"She didn't make many calls," Penelope said.

"But she sent over a hundred texts a day," Joey sighed. "Unfortunately those are more difficult to trace. The content anyway. We can see the numbers she was texting. Lots of friends at her school, her parents, the usual."

"That's a ton of numbers to sort through," Penelope said, shaking her head.

"I know," he said, releasing his side of the report. "Still...see if anything jumps out at you."

She continued to look through the numbers.

"Her computer searches were very focused on Arlena, Max and Randall Madison and any projects they were working on.

She researched Arlena's family like she was doing a term paper on them," Joey said, leafing through the folder again.

"If she thought she was related to them, that's understandable. Did you find any evidence that she was Arlena and Max's sister?"

"We have her birth certificate which states her mother and father are Cheryl and Bradley Anderson, the same parents that she resided with in Lower Manhattan at the time of her death. She was born at Bellevue in 1997. Both of her parents confirm she was their natural daughter, no surrogacy, sperm donor, adoption..." He trailed off, making a circular motion with his hand indicating any other possibility. "They've been together since middle school, the Andersons. Dated all through high school, both went to New York state colleges, and they got married right after they graduated. Holly came along soon afterwards."

"It's so sad. I know teenage girls grow up fast these days, but she still seems like such a baby," Penelope said.

"By all accounts she was a great kid. Did well in school, helped take care of her little brothers. Liked hanging out with her friends, a normal kid." He began organizing the reports again, stacking them into a neater pile. When he lifted them up to tap them on the table to straighten the stack, a picture slid onto the glass. Penelope picked up the photograph and held it by the corner. It was a family portrait of the Andersons, Holly's parents posing behind their three kids, Holly to the left of her twin brothers who looked about six years old in the picture.

"Is this recent?" Penelope asked.

"Yeah, last fall. Holly was fifteen when it was taken," Joey said. He closed the gap between them on the couch and looked at the photo with Penelope.

She felt the warmth coming off of him and fought the urge to lean in. It was getting late and he was looking good. His biceps strained against the fabric of his t-shirt and his torso had that perfect inverted V shape as he leaned back and forth sorting through his reports. Penelope figured she should probably leave before she got herself into trouble. She refocused on the picture in her hand.

"Honestly, I can see where Holly would have questions," Penelope said. "Look at them." She glanced at Joey and held the photo up to shine more light on it. Holly's father was as fair as Penelope, with blond hair and blue eyes and a strong chin on his handsome face. Her mom looked Greek or Italian but was also fair skinned with wavy reddish brown hair. Holly's little brothers were the spitting image of their dad, towheaded boys with blond freckles sprinkled across their noses, different enough to not be identical twins. The boys had wide toothy grins and their mom's hand was draped over one of their shoulders.

And then there was Holly sitting to the left of her brothers, underneath her dad, his hand placed gently on her shoulder. She was dark and beautiful with wide set brown eyes and long black hair. She had the same smile as her mother and there was a similarity in the bridge of their noses, but she was slender and lean where her mom was thicker in the arms and waist. In fact, Holly looked like a fragile bird compared to the rest of her family, who all looked rugged and hearty, like they'd be at home toiling in a potato field.

"I see what you mean," Joey said. "But doesn't every girl fantasize about being someone else? About being related to some long lost famous relative and then becoming famous themselves?"

"Not every girl, I'm sure," Penelope said. "But if Holly had found something out or came across some information that made her think she was Randall Madison's long lost daughter…she seemed to be taking it more seriously than most young girls with a half-baked fantasy of stardom."

"True." Joey looked at the photograph again. "She does resemble Arlena," he said, shrugging.

Penelope picked up the phone records again and pointed to a number. "Who was she calling in Gruver, Texas? Most of these other calls are to LA or New York."

"I noticed that one earlier. It's a company called DIY-DNA." He grabbed his iPhone from the table and tapped the glass, opening the company's website and showing it to her.

"Discreet DNA testing at home," Penelope read from the screen. "Look, you can click there and they'll send you a collection kit."

"So Holly wanted to test her DNA. It does seem she was more than a little curious about all of this."

"If Holly wanted definitive proof that she was related to the Madisons, DNA would be the way to go," Penelope said. "Maybe that's why she came to our house the other night. Could be she was trying to get inside somehow, ask Arlena for a DNA sample or take something from our trash so she could run the test."

"It's a possibility," Joey agreed. He took another sip of wine.

Penelope turned sideways on the couch to face him. "Maybe someone found out she was suspicious and came after her, someone who didn't want her to get a DNA test. But who would kill a young girl because she was trying to prove where she came from?"

"That's the question. It opens up more possibilities," Joey agreed. "I don't like the parents for this though. I can't see either of them leaving her out there in the cold to die alone. Plus, the driver said she was by herself when he dropped her off. Holly's parents are really broken up by all of this. They seem like a close-knit family. Of course we can't rule anything out."

Penelope looked again through the list of phone numbers.

"First I'll find out why she was calling DIY-DNA, see if she was only requesting information or if she was following up on a test. If she got her hands on something of Arlena's from the trash, she might have been calling about the results. Maybe she went to your house to introduce herself as Arlena's long lost sister."

Penelope glanced at Joey's phone which had faded back to his screen saver, a small version of Edvard Munch's *The Scream*. The clock said it was past ten. "I should get going," she said, taking another sip of wine.

"You're welcome to stay as long as you like," Joey said. "Are you hungry? I have some cheese and things I could bring out."

"Oh, no. Don't go to any trouble."

"It's no trouble. It's already put together. Let me grab it. I'd feel better knowing you had something in your stomach." He picked up the bottle of wine and motioned to her, asking silently if she would like some more. She pinched her fingers together in the air to indicate "just a little." He filled her glass halfway again and then topped off his own.

Joey disappeared into the kitchen for a moment and returned with a plate piled high with various cheeses, crackers and grapes. Penelope slid forward to the edge of the couch, crossing her legs and resisting the urge to bounce her foot.

She took a piece of bread and placed a slice of brie on top of it. "You always have a cheese plate at the ready at ten o'clock at night?"

"You never know who might show up." Joey popped a cube of cheddar in his mouth. "How long have you been cooking for the stars?"

Penelope swallowed. "Right out of culinary school, so about seven years. I've always loved movies and I like that every day is different. Plus, I get to be my own boss."

"It suits you. You're out there ordering a bunch of guys around. Like the old days," he teased.

"Excuse me," Penelope leaned back on the couch and crossed her arms over her chest, "but did you just call me bossy?"

"I sure did, Penny Blue. You were always coordinating us into teams to play out in the schoolyard, making up your own rules, eliminating players at will based on your own judgments." Joey chuckled slid closer to her, turning to face her. "You were ruthless."

Penelope laughed out loud and thought it was probably the first time she had in at least a week. "You guys clearly needed someone to take charge and organize your fun for you."

"We did have fun. I remember looking forward to going to school back then, for the playing, not so much for the learning. I always looked forward to seeing you." Joey placed his hand lightly on her shoulder. "You were always nice to me, even when it wasn't popular to be nice to the fat kid."

Penelope wasn't sure if it was the wine or Joey's sudden openness, but it felt like it was much warmer in his apartment than it had been ten minutes earlier. Her cheeks flushed.

"Kids are jerks sometimes. You know that. You were always cool and funny. Everyone saw that once they got to know you," Penelope said, taking his other hand in hers, entwining his fingers and laying it lightly on her thigh.

"But you didn't wait to get to know me. You were nice from the get go, gave me a chance. You didn't care about what anybody thought." Joey searched her face, a faint smile of remembrance on his lips.

Penelope glanced down, embarrassed and at a loss for words. She had no idea how Joey must have felt back then, being on the outside looking in. She didn't remember it being that way for him, but she guessed you never knew how others were really feeling, especially during those awkward preteen years. When she glanced back up, Joey was looking right into her eyes, still smiling. He leaned towards her and pulled her close, and hugging her tightly. He whispered into her ear, "I've never forgotten that about you, Penny Blue."

A shiver shot through her body and she hugged him back, closing her eyes and breathing in his scent. His breath was hot against her neck, and he lingered there, smelling her hair. Penelope wasn't sure she could keep herself from grabbing him by the shirt, throwing him down on the couch and violently making out with him if he kept this up. She savored the closeness of him for three beats longer then pulled away saying, "I should probably go." She was proud of herself for keeping the shakiness out of her voice. She was cool as a cucumber on the outside but inside she was melting like candle wax.

"Are you okay to drive?" Joey reluctantly pulled away and relaxed back onto the couch. "I can take you home if you're tired."

"That's sweet," Penelope said, smoothing her hands down her thighs, readying herself to stand up from the soft leather couch. "It's been a crazy week but I got a lot of sleep yesterday. Thank you for the offer."

"Anytime." He let out a long sigh, bringing himself back from their shared moment. "Thanks for coming. You helped me out tonight and I appreciate it."

"No problem. I hope you can figure out who did this," Penelope said. They both stood up at the same time, Penelope grabbing their empty wine glasses and heading towards the kitchen.

"You don't have to clean up."

"It's no problem. Force of habit. You hand wash these or do they go in the dishwasher?"

Joey was gathering up the cheese tray and crackers and said to her over his shoulder, "I put them in the dishwasher. It's got a special gentle cycle for winos like me with lots of glasses."

Penelope opened the dishwasher. It was empty except for two plates stacked next to each other on the bottom rack. She pulled out the top rack and saw two more wine glasses that matched the ones in her hand. As she placed the glasses in the rack and slid it back into place, a glimmer of pink caught her eye. She pulled the rack back out to look again, glancing over her shoulder first to see if Joey was nearby. Seeing she was still alone in the kitchen, she took a closer look and her mood dipped. Along the rim of one of the glasses was an imprint of frosted pink lipstick. Penelope straightened up and slid the rack slowly back into place.

They said their goodbyes and Joey saw her to the door.

"I'll be in touch," Joey said, patting his pockets as if he was trying to remember something. "Maybe we can do this again sometime."

"Sure." Penelope brushed invisible lint off of her shoulder. The image of the frosted pink lipstick wine glass danced around her head. She opened the door. "Bye, Joey."

"I'll call you tomorrow. About the lip gloss."

CHAPTER 14

Penelope walked through the back door of her house and into the kitchen twenty minutes later. She entered her passcode on the alarm keypad and dropped her bag onto the antique coat stand to the right of the door. Shrugging out of her coat, she hung it on one of the black iron hooks.

Sam's Hummer was parked in the driveway. Most of the lights were off on Arlena's side of the house so she assumed she and Sam were upstairs asleep. Penelope contemplated going upstairs and falling into her own bed. She was tired and relaxed from the wine at Joey's place, but at the same time her mind was agitated from the visit.

"Pen is back," Max whispered dramatically, suddenly entering the kitchen from the hallway.

Penelope jumped. "Max!"

He held his hands up in the air in mock surrender. "Sorry. I thought you heard me coming. What are you up to? Home from a hot date?"

"The question is what are you up to? Lurking around the house, jumping out at people?" They both kept their voices low.

"I'm getting ready to watch a movie. Want to join me?"

"I'm tired. I don't know."

"I'll make popcorn," he said.

Penelope wavered. "Okay. But nothing scary." Maybe a movie would help her unwind and take her mind off of Joey.

"You got it," Max said. "Go get comfy. I'll meet you in the library in ten minutes."

Penelope went up to her room, pulling her sweater up over her head as she slowly climbed the stairs. When she got to her bedroom she peeled off her jeans and laid her clothes on the large chaise lounge near her window. She made a mental note to drop the borrowed clothes at the cleaners before returning them to Kelley. She slipped off her bra and pulled on a black cotton tank top and grey yoga pants.

She pulled her hair up into a high ponytail as she went back down the stairs, and padded barefoot into the library. Max was sitting on one end of the couch. When he saw her come in he patted the cushion next to him, inviting her to come over and sit. He'd made a big bowl of popcorn which sat on the large slate coffee table next to an open bottle of wine and two glasses. There was a fire in the fireplace and a scented pillar candle burning on the far end of the table.

"More wine," Penelope said. "I've already had half a bottle tonight."

"So it *was* a hot date," Max teased. He grabbed the bottle and poured some in a glass, handing it to Penelope. "Here you go, beautiful. Unless you'd prefer some champagne?"

Penelope rolled her eyes. "No thanks. And it wasn't a hot date." She took a sip and looked at the DVDs Max had fanned out on the table in front of them. She loved this room. It was full of comfortable couches and chairs, decorated in a modern style in soothing camel and burgundy tones, the walls lined with bookcases. A huge flat screen TV hung on the far wall which could be hidden behind a sliding book case when not in use. "Let's watch this one," she said, picking up and waving the case for *Soapdish*.

"Whatever the lady desires," Max said, taking the case from her. He pushed himself up from the couch and slid the disc into the DVD player that sat on a clear glass shelf beneath the TV. When he sat back down he pulled a small wicker basket out from underneath the end table nearest him which held various remotes. He selected one of them and pressed some buttons, bringing the screen and then the player to life. Previews began to roll across the screen.

"Surround sound?" Max asked, selecting a smaller, white remote.

"Sure, why not? They can't hear anything way up there," Penelope said, glancing towards the other side of the house.

"She's also got some medicinal help tonight." Max winked. He activated the hidden speakers and rich sound filled the room.

"Did she seem okay when she got home?" Penelope asked.

"I think so. She was bumming because of her lips being all puffy and from everything that happened on set," Max said. "Arlena's tough, though. She'll be fine in the morning."

"You're a good brother, Max. I know Arlena really cares about you."

"I wish we had grown up together. It would have been cool to have a big sister like her looking out for me." He grabbed the bowl of popcorn and settled back on the couch.

"How's your mom?" Penelope asked, taking a sip of wine.

"She's fine. She and her boyfriend are doing the hippie commune thing out there in Oregon. Living off the land, smoking weed. They're happy."

Penelope looked at the screen then back at Max. He was handsome in an easy-going, relaxed way. His cheekbones were high and sharp and he always looked like he was about to break into a smile. He was wearing black track pants and a soft red t-shirt with thick white socks on his feet. Turning sideways on the couch, she drew her legs up under her and reached into the bowl for some popcorn. The movie menu screen came on and Max selected Play.

He winked at her. "I get to host the second half of your date night, looks like."

Penelope groaned. "It wasn't a date. It was a visit with the detective who is working on Holly Anderson's murder case."

"A visit with a police detective and you had wine?"

Penelope sighed. "Yeah, but we used to be friends, we went to school together when we were kids. Anyway, I'm pretty sure he had another date right before I got there."

Max raised his eyebrows. "A double feature? Looks like everyone is doubling up tonight. You think the detective's a player?"

"I don't know. Maybe. I'm pretty sure there was someone there with him when I called. Then I saw two dishes in the dishwasher and a wine glass with lipstick on it. Like he'd had dinner with someone. Ugly pink frosty lipstick," Penelope added under her breath, reaching again into the popcorn bowl. "It's not like we're dating. Not even close. The man can have dinner with someone." She put the handful of popcorn in her mouth.

"Wait, did you invite yourself over to his place?" Max asked.

"Not really...I called to talk to him about what happened today and he asked me to stop by. I had something for him, something to do with what happened with Arlena, and he asked me to drop it by on my way home."

"Well, it sounds like he got rid of the pink lipstick lady when he knew you were coming over," Max said, sipping his wine. "If I make dinner for a girl at my place I usually don't want her to leave right after, if you know what I mean."

Penelope contemplated that as they both turned their attention to the screen.

After a few minutes, Max turned the volume down and said,

"What did he say about the girl?" He nodded towards the street in front of the house.

Penelope laid her head against the back of the couch. "He thinks she was trying to prove she was related to you. That maybe she thought she was your sister."

"Oh, man." Max shook his head and ran his hand through his unruly black hair. "I remember when I finally met Dad. I was five and he came and took me and my mom out to dinner. Stayed with us for a week. It was awesome. He took me to the zoo and we camped out in a tent in the backyard. Lots of fun stuff." Max looked down into the bowl of popcorn. "Then he had to go, flew off to Helsinki to film a movie for six months. There were other visits and he took care of me and my mom. Always sent money, gifts on my birthday, Christmas, you know. That week was the best, though."

"It's nice you guys are close now. All of you."

"But if Holly Anderson was really Holly Madison, I didn't know about her. Dad never mentioned the name Holly to me. I heard about Arlena growing up. And Anthony, our brother in Texas. He's still a kid, about twelve now, I think. And we have another ten-year-old sister in California named Saffron, but she's never been in contact with us."

"Do you know of any others?" Penelope stifled a yawn.

"No, but Dad's been making movies for thirty years everywhere in the world. I guess anything is possible. I might have a sister in Helsinki." He chuckled.

Penelope nodded, took a sip of wine and placed her glass back on the table. "Hand me that blanket?" she asked, pointing to a soft cashmere throw on the back of the couch. It was the same deep caramel color as the furniture. Max handed it to her and she draped it over her legs, turning her attention back to the movie.

"Penny," a warm whisper tickled her ear.

"Hmm…" Penelope mumbled sleepily.

"You want me to take you to bed?" Max whispered to her.

Penelope's eyes sprang open and she saw movie credits crawling up the big screen. The room was lit by the candle and the TV, the fire having died down to embers. The wine bottle stood empty next to the half-empty bowl of popcorn.

"Sure. You can take me to bed," Penelope said wearily. "I can't get up. I'm exhausted." She closed her eyes again, drifting back to sleep.

Max flipped off the TV. He blew out the candle and scooped her up off of the couch, carrying her easily in his long muscular arms. Penelope curled into him, resting her head on his shoulder as he made his way out of the library, up the stairs and into her bedroom. By the time they got to her room Penelope was dozing off again. Max pulled back her soft down-filled comforter and laid her gently down on the bed, leaning over her to arrange the sheets over her. Penelope rolled onto her side, tucking her arm under her pillow and snuggling it to her face. She reached up and placed a hand on Max's cheek. "Thanks, Max," she whispered.

Max pulled Penelope's comforter up to her shoulder and smoothed a strand of her hair back over her ear. He hesitated a minute and then leaned down, kissing her lightly on the cheek.

"Good night, Pen." He stepped quietly from the room, turning off the light switch as he left.

CHAPTER 15

Rumbling thunder mixed with Zazoo's barrage of piercing barks woke Penelope the next morning. She opened her eyes, saw bright sunshine peeking through the blinds and wondered how it could be thundering. She'd been dreaming about Joey. For some reason they were having a dinner party at Joey's mother's house and Penelope had brought Irish soda bread. Joey's mother had never heard of it. Penelope was trying to explain why it was called soda bread, but Joey's mom kept nodding and not understanding, responding to her only in Italian. They were eating outside under a pergola in a huge sweeping backyard that looked more like Napa Valley or Sicily. Penelope was sure Joey's real backyard growing up was only a small patch of grass like hers had been behind the attached brownstones that lined Mott Street. He had lived on one end of the street and she on the other when they were in grade school. Penelope hadn't been on Mott Street since her parents packed up and moved to Florida right after she graduated from high school.

The rumbling ended abruptly and Penelope realized it was a car engine outside her window, not thunder.

She sat up in bed and stretched her arms lazily over her head. She heard a low mumble of sleepy voices downstairs and then the front door opening. Then the voices became more animated. Penelope rolled out of bed and made her way to her adjoining bathroom. She took a peek out of the window and saw a shiny black Shelby Mustang with Pennsylvania license plates parked behind Sam's Hummer in the driveway.

Penelope followed the voices into the kitchen as she made her way downstairs. When she entered the room she saw Sam sitting at the kitchen island smiling at Randall Madison, who was holding Arlena up in the air in a bear hug, Zazoo tap dancing around his feet.

"There's my baby girl." Randall Madison's smoky voice was deep and gravelly. He was at least six foot four and he held Arlena up in the air effortlessly.

"Daddy, I'm so glad you're here."

Randall set her back down but kept her in a tight hug, Arlena disappearing behind his thick arms. "How are you doing, pumpkin?" He pulled away to look at her face.

"I'm good, Daddy. When did you get back?"

He continued to study her face, then glanced over at Sam. "I just got here. Drove all night from Pittsburgh after we wrapped," he said, his New Jersey accent clipping through his words. "Max called, said there was some trouble. You're hurt?" Concern pinched his handsome face.

"I'm better now." Arlena reached over and grabbed Sam's hand. They were both dressed in warm flannel pajamas and looked well rested. Arlena's lips had gone back to their normal size, still full and puffy but as they should be, not overblown by her allergies. Her skin was once again healthy and radiant looking.

"Good morning, Pen," Max said quietly into her ear as he snuck up behind her and made his way into the kitchen. "You made good time, huh, Dad?" Max and Randall hugged each other roughly, swaying on their feet. Max was slightly shorter and thinner than his dad, but you could tell they were father and son by their similar builds and shiny black hair.

"Five hours on the road. The shoot is over and I've got a few weeks before the next one," he said, glancing at Penelope. Zazoo sat at attention, staring up at Randall.

"Hi, Mr. Madison, I'm Penelope." She walked towards him with her hand extended.

Randall Madison looked down at her and took her small hand in his large one, his hardened features softening around his eyes. "Penelope, I've heard a lot about you." He bent down and kissed her knuckles.

"All good things, I hope," Penelope stammered. She figured she was still back in her dream world because iconic film legend Randall Madison was kissing her hand in her own kitchen.

"Excellent things. Thanks for looking out for Arlena. Max said you were there for her when she got sick on set. I won't forget that." He let go of Penelope's hand and pulled her into a hug, crushing her against his chest. His jacket smelled like burnt cherry cigar smoke, pleasant and manly.

Penelope felt the crushing weight of his arms on her. She pulled out of the hug and noticed everyone was watching them. Suddenly self-conscious, she announced, "Who's hungry?"

"I am," Sam said loudly.

"What are we all in the mood for?"

"Pancakes. Definitely pancakes," Sam said.

"Sounds good," Penelope said. She went to the stove and began pulling some pans out of the neighboring cabinet.

"Sam Cavanaugh," Randall said. He walked over to Sam and slapped him heartily on the back. He then pulled off his leather jacket and handed it to Max. "Hang this up for me, will ya, kiddo?"

"Sure, Dad." Max took the heavy jacket and hung it on one of the iron hooks by the door.

"Randall Madison. Nice to meet you, sir," Sam said, shaking his hand firmly.

Randall slid onto the stool next to Sam. Penelope glanced over and saw the two men sizing each other up. Randall was dark and lean in contrast with Sam's muscular California Golden Boy looks.

Max moved behind the island to Penelope's side and draped his arm across her shoulders. "Can I help?" he leaned down to ask.

"Sure. Grab me some lemons and there's a package of blueberries in the crisper. And get the cinnamon sticks and vanilla beans from the pantry."

"Will do." He winked at her and moved towards the pantry. Penelope blushed, suddenly remembering Max carrying her up the stairs the night before. She glanced quickly at his back as he stood surveying the pantry items and then flipped on the gas range. Blue flames licked the bottoms of the skillets.

"So it looks like you two are enjoying working together on Sal's movie," Randall said, shifting on his stool. He was still facing Sam, looking directly at him as he addressed both him and Arlena.

"We are. Right, babe?" Sam said, putting his arm around Arlena. She stood next to his stool, keeping some space between herself and Sam. Penelope noticed Arlena was acting stiffly, a big difference from the last few days of being stuck like glue to Sam's side. Maybe she didn't want to be too affectionate in front of her dad. They'd been caught together in their pajamas, so there was no denying they were friends...close friends.

"We are, Daddy," she said. "Sam's been a rock during everything...the shoot, rehearsals, and everything else."

"It's nothing." Sam pulled her again into his side. "I like being there for you."

Penelope began to whisk pancake batter in a large yellow

bowl on the opposite side of the island. She kept her gaze downward, focusing on the food, trying to give them as much privacy as possible. Which wasn't much. Zazoo went to sit on his bed but kept his eyes trained on everyone at the counter.

"Are you together now? Or did you invite yourself to sleep over because of what happened to Arlena yesterday?" Randall asked, his focus still on Sam.

Max turned halfway around from his place in front of the pantry and Penelope stopped whisking. All attention turned to Arlena and Sam.

"Daddy!" Arlena said, pulling away from Sam.

"What? I'm just asking. You guys look really...comfortable together, is all."

"Arlena is a great girl, Mr. Madison," Sam said, still pulling a resisting Arlena towards him.

"That's right, Sam. That's something you shouldn't forget," Randall said. He picked up a stray paper clip off of the counter and began to bend it out of shape.

"You don't have to worry about that, sir," Sam said. Penelope couldn't tell if Sam was intimidated by Randall or not. He seemed like he was trying to be respectful...as respectful as you can be in your pajamas fresh out of bed with a man's daughter.

"Arlena is a grown woman, very capable and smart. I'm not worried about her." Randall twisted the paperclip between his thick fingers. "But I'd worry about you, Sam, if Arlena gets hurt by you in this." He finished twisting the clip and laid it down on the counter, folding his hands together.

Penelope and Max went back to making the pancakes. Penelope realized she still hadn't talked to Arlena about her relationship with Sam, but assumed they must be together by now. But then she supposed it didn't matter one way or another, as long as they were happy. She handed the bowl of batter to

Max and he began ladling circles of batter into the hot pans. Penelope rinsed the blueberries that she would mix with sugar and cinnamon as a topping for the pancakes.

"I love Sam very much," Arlena said suddenly and clearly to no one in particular.

Once again, all movement stopped in the room and everyone looked at Arlena. Sam smiled knowingly at her and pulled her onto his lap. "I love you too." They kissed lightly on the lips.

Randall said, "That settles that then."

Beyoncé's "Crazy in Love" played loudly from the corner of the kitchen where Arlena and Penelope charged their phones.

"Oh, that's my phone," Arlena said, bounding behind the island to answer it.

"Subtle ring tone, sis." Max chuckled, flipping perfectly golden pancakes to finish the other sides.

"Shut up, Max," Arlena said. "Hello?" she said into the phone. "Oh, hi Sal."

The others fell silent, listening to Arlena's side of the conversation and Sal's muted responses from the phone.

"I appreciate that, Sal. Thanks for calling...yes, I'm good now. Nothing to worry about."

Arlena shifted her weight from one foot to the other, the hand not holding the phone nervously twisting a strand of her hair.

"Tomorrow? Um..." She glanced at Randall. "I'd love to, Sal, but my father is in town and my brother is also visiting."

The murmuring grew louder and Penelope heard Sal laughing on the other end of the line.

"I'll find out if they can and let you know before tomorrow," Arlena said. "And I'm sorry if I've delayed us..."

Penelope distinctly heard Sal cut in. "No way. You're doing great and everything is fine."

"Thanks for saying that, Sal. I'll be in touch about dinner. Bye." Arlena touched the screen to end her call and slid onto the stool next to her dad.

"Sal has invited all of us to dinner at his house tomorrow," Arlena said to them. "I told him you were in town, Daddy, and he said he hopes you'll come too."

Randall said, "Sunday dinner at Sal Marco's house? I wouldn't miss it. He's famous for those. Back in the old days we would meet every Sunday...all the actors and writers, some of the crew...we'd eat, drink and talk about whatever project we were on. One of Sal's morale boosting tactics."

Max slid pancakes onto a platter on the counter.

Penelope eased up beside him and placed ramekins of cinnamon and blueberry infused syrup next to them and a stack of plates for them to serve themselves. "Max, these look delicious."

"They were made with love. It was easy." Max reached down and patted her lightly on the behind.

Penelope froze, her cheeks flaring pink. She knew he was just being Max but this crossed the line.

Penelope had fought off a few gropers in culinary school and that behavior always set her on edge. As Max leaned over to hand out plates across the island she patted him back, right in the same place.

"Whoa. Thanks, Pen."

"Max, knock it off," Arlena said. "Seriously, I love you, but grow up."

Sam and Randall chuckled as they dug into their pancakes, focusing on their plates.

"Sal's going to call and invite you too, Sam." Arlena leaned forward and talked across Randall. "I don't know why I didn't tell him you were here," she added quietly.

"It's fine, Arlena," Sam said after swallowing a mouthful of pancake. "He's the boss but we don't have to tell anyone anything until we're ready."

"He invited you too, Pen." Arlena stabbed a pancake and quickly transferred it to her plate before the fork gave up its hold.

"That a surprise. I thought he'd still be angry with me about yesterday. The last time I saw Sal he was yelling at me."

"Salvatore is all bark, very little bite," Randall said, not looking up from his plate. "Plus, he wants everyone to be happy and get along. A happy crew is easier to work with. Maybe he wants to apologize to you, Penelope."

"He doesn't need to do that," Penelope said.

"If you weren't there," Randall continued, "it might have ended differently, with Arlena in the hospital. You stopped it before it got really bad. He should be thanking you."

"Thanks, Mr. Madison," Penelope said, finally pulling a pancake onto a plate for herself after she was sure everyone had enough.

"It's Randall. And these pancakes are delicious, son. Good to know you know how to use your hands for more than one thing."

Max made a face at him and took a sip of coffee.

"So it's agreed. Dinner at Sal's tomorrow," Randall said, pushing back from his plate. "Just like the old days."

CHAPTER 16

Max helped Penelope clean up after breakfast. He loaded dishes and glasses into the dishwasher while she washed the utensils and bowls in the deep stainless sink. Arlena and Sam had gone to her room to get dressed for the day and Randall, after retrieving a large duffel bag from his Mustang, was unpacking his clothes in one of the larger guest rooms.

"Tasty pancakes," Max said.

"They sure were. Thanks for helping," Penelope agreed. "So I guess that's it then. Sam and Arlena are together."

"It was kind of obvious, I suppose," he said, shrugging. "I like him better than Vance. When she was with him he always made me feel like an intruder." He finished loading the machine and closed the door. "It's good she's happy, you know?" He wiped his hands on a dish towel.

"It seems mutual, which is good for both of them. It's never good when the affection is only one sided," Penelope said. She turned off the water and took the towel from him, drying her hands also.

"I suppose. So what do you have planned for today, Pen?"

"Not sure yet. I never know what to do with myself when I have a big stretch of free time."

"You're always working. It's time to relax," Max said. He grabbed her hand and twirled her around in a circle then pulled her close and they swayed for a second in front of the sink.

Penelope pushed him away gently. "Oh yeah, and before...with the butt slap thing?" Penelope perched a hand on her hip and looked sternly at him as he continued to sway to the music in his head. "Unless you're invited, this is a hands-off zone," she said motioning at her behind.

Max stopped swaying and his face became serious. "You're right, Pen. Absolutely right. I will wait until I'm invited, and until then I will dream about your hands-off zone." He grabbed her hands and began to sway with her again.

Penelope pushed him away playfully. "Max, you're impossible."

"No, I can be difficult at times but I'm totally possible." He spun her around in a twirl. Penelope let herself sway with him for a moment longer.

Finally she said, "You're right about one thing. I am going to relax today. Starting with a long bath upstairs." She broke away from him and headed towards the hall and the staircase beyond.

"Sounds good. You enjoy yourself. If you want some company yell and I'll be right up..." Max called after her.

Penelope started the bath water and pulled off her pajamas. She poured two drops of lavender scented oil into the steamy water and lowered herself down, closing her eyes and slouching so the water came up over her shoulders. Penelope attempted to clear her mind, trying her best to think of nothing, focusing only on the hot water loosening her muscles. But eventually her thoughts turned to Holly Anderson. She grimaced as she pushed the image of Holly's pretty frozen face out of her mind and focused instead on the other pictures she'd seen of her, when she was an alive and vibrant young girl. Now that she'd met Randall Madison in person, she tried to compare his face with Holly's.

Then she thought about Joey and a smile spread across her lips. She kept her eyes closed and pictured him from the night before in his tight t-shirt, whispering in her ear. Then she frowned, remembering the lipstick on the wine glass and her stiff goodbye to him. Rolling her eyes internally, Penelope shifted in the tub and tried to bring her thoughts back to a neutral place. She wasn't doing a good job of relaxing. Her mind at least. Her body felt like it had turned to lead in the water.

Just then her phone buzzed in the bedroom. The door to the bathroom was slightly open and her phone was on her vanity table.

The sun streamed through the windows and Penelope guessed it was probably around eleven. The bath water had turned tepid and she decided to get out and see who was calling, hoping it wasn't anything work related.

She wrapped herself in a large white towel and padded into the bedroom onto the soft carpet, grabbing her phone off of the vanity as she went. She sat on the bed and opened the screen. "Joey: missed call & voicemail" blinked back at her.

She lightly tossed the phone onto the bed, standing up and letting the towel drop to the floor. She pulled on a pair of comfortable jeans and a long sleeved t-shirt before listening to the voicemail. She pulled the soft rubber band slowly from her ponytail as she listened.

"Penny, hi, it's Joey. I'd like to come by later today and speak with you and Arlena if that's possible. Give me a call back and let me know. Thanks and have a good day."

Penelope pulled the phone away from her ear and stared at the screen. Suddenly Joey, the one with the wine and cheese from last night, was all business. She listened to the message again and then slipped her phone into her back pocket and headed downstairs.

Everyone was gathered in the library, lounging in front of the lit fireplace. Sam and Arlena sat almost on top of each other on one end of the sofa and Max and Randall sat in the matching club chairs that flanked it. Zazoo happily chewed on a thin rawhide stick under the coffee table. The TV was covered up by the sliding bookcase and they were all looking at a scrapbook that was open on the square slate coffee table. Randall was flipping the pages and pointing out different pictures and articles to them. Penelope stopped in the doorway, debating whether or not to interrupt them. She rapped lightly on the door frame to get their attention.

"There you are. We're looking at some old stuff from when I worked with Sal. Some of them go way back...before these two were even a glimmer." Randall winked at Max.

"Oh, I don't want to intrude on you guys," Penelope said.

"Pen, please, don't be silly. Sit down," Arlena said, patting the couch cushion next to her.

"Thanks," Penelope said, taking a seat.

"This was one of the first movies I made with Sal," Randall said, pointing to a black and white photograph. In it Randall was shirtless, his hair cut in a military style buzz cut, his eyes wild and glassy with tears.

"*The Private Army*, right Dad?" Max said.

"Yep. Filmed that one out in Brooklyn. Low budget, which is Sal's middle name. This was his first three-week shoot. Back then it was because he had no money and he was trying to film as many projects as possible. Now he's become known for those...and for his big blockbusters, of course."

Arlena nodded. "It means so much that he called me for this, Daddy. I was afraid I would never get off the B-movie path."

Randall gazed lovingly at his daughter. "You're starting out, proving yourself. I know you've got what it takes. Now you'll have a chance to show everyone. Sal's good at finding diamonds in the rough like you and me."

Arlena sighed. "I appreciate that. It's hard because you take jobs when you're starting out because you need the work and the credits, but then you get pigeonholed as only being that one thing. I was terrified I'd never break out and no one would take me seriously until Sal called."

"You're doing fine. Peter's a solid agent and he's going to get you on the right path," Randall said.

"I hope so. I've got this movie right now but nothing after it lined up. This is my big break. If it doesn't do well, I'm not sure what will happen. I can't go back to working for Brett either. That bridge is burned."

"Who's Brett?" Randall asked sharply.

"The *Slash 'Em* director, Brett Ralston. He said I'd never work again after I walked off that movie. I don't feel comfortable with on screen nudity. I'm not sure I'll ever be." She glanced at Sam, who nodded.

"Screw him," Randall said, an edge coming into his voice. "He makes threats against my little girl, he'll be sorry. I promise you that."

"Daddy, I don't want to work with him anyway."

"That's not the point. He doesn't know who he's dealing with. Anyone tries to hurt either of you," he pointed at Max and Arlena, "you let me know. Some of these snot-nosed young directors working today don't know their asses from Fellini. They're living in the house that I helped build."

An uneasy silence fell across the group.

"Working for scale barely covered the bills when I was starting out. But we all did it to be part of something with Sal," Randall's tone became lighter, his anger momentarily forgotten as he glanced back down at the image of his younger self.

Randall flipped a page in the book and unfolded a yellowing article that had been taped next to a couple of movie stubs. "This is the *New York Times* review of the movie," Randall said. "A rave. Called Sal a genius which he is. But he was new on the scene then. We all were."

"You could find that review online in the archives of the *Times*, Dad," Max said. "Probably a bunch of pictures of the shoot too."

"Let me ask you something, kiddo. You have a scrapbook? Anything where you keep a history of your achievements? Photos? Articles about yourself?"

"No, Dad. I can find all of that stuff online," Max said with playful impatience.

"That's true, son. I'm sure you can. But what happens when the electricity goes out? Then you have nothing," Randall said, closing the scrapbook.

"Daddy, leave that here for a bit. I want to see more of it," Arlena said.

"I'll be back in a while," Randall said, standing up and stretching. "But I'm taking you all out to dinner tonight."

Penelope turned to Arlena. "Joey...Detective Baglioni...left me a message saying he wanted to ask us some more questions."

"Oh," Arlena said, deflating a bit. "Today?"

"Yeah," Penelope said. "I met with him last night and he has a few new leads he's working on. Both with Holly and with, well..." She sighed, glancing away from Arlena. Gathering herself, she began again. "Something made me think what happened to you on set yesterday wasn't an accident. Kelley and I think someone might have messed with your makeup, so I took it to Joey. I planned to tell you this morning, but with everyone here it didn't seem the right time."

Arlena's eyes took on a hard edge. "What do you mean 'messed with', Pen?"

"Someone might have tampered with your makeup, used it to trigger an allergic reaction."

"Are you saying that someone is intentionally trying to hurt me?"

Penelope placed her hand on Arlena's upper arm. "I don't know, Arlena. But I'm worried about you. A girl gets murdered outside our house, and then there are two separate incidents with you on set this week? I mean, it's hard to think that's all a coincidence. What if someone really is trying to hurt you?"

CHAPTER 17

The front doorbell rang just before seven. Penelope's heart skipped as she put aside her iPad, hopped off the kitchen island stool and headed to the front door. She'd been surfing recipe sites and making notes for menu ideas while she waited for everyone else to get ready for dinner, and for Joey to stop by.

Joey was on the front porch in a blue suit and a long wool coat. "Detective, nice to see you again," Penelope said, showing him inside.

"Likewise, Penny."

She led him through the foyer and down the hallway to the kitchen. "Would you like a cup of coffee?"

"No, thank you. You look nice."

Penelope flushed and glanced away, still trying to balance Joey's formality mixed with familiarity routine. She was dressed for dinner in tight black slacks, black mid-calf leather riding boots and a shimmery beige silk top. She knew she looked good, better than he'd seen her lately.

Sam wandered into the kitchen from the opposite hallway, dressed for dinner in a black suit with a crisp white shirt opened at the collar. He took a beer from the fridge and sat on a stool at the island.

"Detective. Working on Saturday?" Sam said, taking a swig of beer.

"That happens a lot. I've got some information and a couple of questions for Arlena."

"She'll be out in a minute."

The back door opened, letting in a gust of cold air and a whiff of cigar smoke. Randall and Max came inside, Randall's arm draped heavily over his son's shoulders. They were laughing, but when they saw Joey they paused. "Who do we have here?" Randall asked as he eyed Joey up and down, giving Max's shoulders one more squeeze before releasing him.

"Mr. Madison, I'm Detective Joseph Baglioni. Penelope mentioned on the phone you were in town. I'm investigating the homicide of a young girl in the neighborhood." He extended his hand for Randall to shake.

"So you're the detective I've been hearing about," Randall said, shaking Joey's hand. "This is my son, Max." He released Joey's hand and nodded towards Max. "I gather you know Penelope already."

"Yes, sir. Penelope and I go back a ways. We were friends in grade school."

"Is that right?" Randall asked. He walked to the refrigerator and grabbed two beers, holding one out for Joey. "Small world."

"No thank you," Joey said, waving away the bottle.

Randall handed it to Max, who twisted off the cap. He stood behind Penelope's, resting his hand on the back of her stool.

Arlena entered the kitchen and, as usual, all attention turned to her. She was dressed in skin tight cream leather pants and a transparent black silk shirt with a sleek black camisole underneath. She had on short cuffed leather boots with toe cut outs, a red toenail showing through on each foot. Her long black hair hung in a shiny wave down her back. Her lips were a deep red, but otherwise she wore minimal makeup and no jewelry.

"Miss Madison, thank you for taking the time to talk with me," Joey said.

"Oh...hello, Detective," Arlena said, momentarily startled when she saw Joey standing in the kitchen. Since their big revelation at breakfast, Arlena and Sam had been pretty focused on each other, everything else taking a backseat.

"Is there somewhere we can speak privately?" Joey asked, glancing at the others in the room.

Arlena sighed. "That's not necessary, Detective. This is my family. Go ahead."

Joey paused for a moment before continuing. "The reason I wanted to talk to you was to let you know that Penelope was right. Someone tampered with your makeup."

Penelope's heart sank even though she had suspected as much. "The lip gloss was tainted with something?"

"It appears the tubes were laced with seafood residue. For someone with a severe allergy like yourself, it was enough to make you very ill."

Sam stepped behind Arlena and placed a protective hand on her shoulder. Arlena remained still and stared at Joey.

"Can you think of any reason someone would do that?" Joey asked.

"Of course not..." she trailed off, her gaze wandering. "I honestly can't think of anyone who would go out of their way to hurt me."

"It doesn't necessarily have to be someone she knows," Randall said. "There are lots of crazy people out there. Maybe some nut has become fixated on Arlena."

"That's a possibility, Mr. Madison. But we also have to consider that it's someone close to your daughter, someone holding a grudge against her, for something real or imagined."

"How am I supposed to know if someone has an imagined grudge against me?" Arlena asked, a touch of impatience in her voice.

"That's what I'm asking you to think about. An incident that may seem like nothing to you could have upset an unstable acquaintance or fan. If you've had any run-ins lately that didn't feel right or a minor altercation...anything like that would be helpful to remember."

Penelope glanced at Arlena as she tried to think. Arlena was always professional on the set, and she didn't remember anything like what Joey was describing. Arlena could be a bit of a diva at times, but nothing over the top. Certainly nothing anyone would want to killer her over.

"What about that Brett asshole?" Randall asked Arlena.

"Brett? Daddy, we had a disagreement about work. I've known him for years, filmed three movies with him. He would never try to physically hurt me."

"His movie tanked without you," Sam said, rubbing her shoulder. "Maybe he is holding a grudge against you for walking off."

"It's true," she said to Sam, "that things didn't end well between us. But poisoning me over it? I don't think he'd do that."

"Who are you talking about?" Joey asked, flipping his pad open to take notes.

"Brett Ralston. R-A-L-S-T-O-N," Randall said, punctuating the letters with his pointed finger. "He's a no-talent director who tried to take advantage of Arlena, and then threatened her when she wouldn't take her clothes off for his piece of crap movie."

Joey jotted the name down. When he finished he looked up and said, "Mr. Madison, have you ever heard the name Holly Anderson?"

Randall shook his head and took a swig of beer. "Doesn't ring a bell, Detective."

"How about Cheryl or Bradley Anderson?"

"I've met a few Cheryls and a lot of Brads in my day. Anything about them that stands out?"

"Their daughter might have been trying to prove she was your daughter. Their names mean anything to you now?" Joey asked.

Max shifted uncomfortably on his feet behind Penelope. Joey looked at Max and Penelope saw the familiar muscle twitch in his jaw.

"Detective, I love my kids." He spread his arms wide, motioning around the room at the others. "I take care of every single one of them. If she was my daughter, I didn't know about it."

Joey pulled some pictures from his inside coat pocket. He sorted through them quickly then held up one of Holly's headshots for Randall to see. "Recognize her?"

Randall took the picture from Joey and held it at an angle to shine more light on it. "No. Pretty girl, though." He handed the picture back to Joey.

Joey handed him another photo, this time the family portrait. "How about her?" Joey asked, indicating Cheryl Anderson.

Randall smiled knowingly. "Now her I remember. What did you say her name was?"

"Cheryl," Joey said.

"I don't remember her name being Cheryl, but I remember her face," Randall said. "I worked on a movie, a sci-fi flick called *Outward Invasion*, and I met her," he tapped the photo, "on the last day. She was working the after party, serving drinks."

"Daddy," Arlena said with a heavy sigh.

Randall handed the picture back to Joey. "Look, we hooked up. We were together one time and I never heard from her again. I certainly never heard of Holly or any other child until right this minute. You know if I had I would have told you guys, and I would have taken care of them."

"You say her name wasn't Cheryl?" Joey asked.

"It was something else. Rachel, I think," Randall said. "Look, it was a long time ago. But I never forget a face and that face belonged to Rachel, definitely not Cheryl."

Max and Arlena remained silent, staring at their father.

Joey cleared his throat, cutting the awkward silence. "If Holly wanted to, how would she go about getting in touch with you, Mr. Madison?"

"One of the assistants in my manager's office handles my correspondence, emails, calls, that kind of thing. It's mostly people pitching screenplays or requesting appearances, that kind of thing. They brief me on what comes in, and they keep a file on anything off the wall or threatening. I'm contacted by hundreds of people, but they would know to bring something like a claim about a long lost child to my attention. You can check with them about Holly, see if she tried to contact me."

"Actually, we determined through her computer search that Holly emailed you last month," Joey said, flipping again through his leather bound pad. "She didn't mention her mother or her suspicions about your relationship to her. It looks like she was trying to set up a meeting with you."

"They must have filed it away as a fan letter," Randall said, shaking his head. "I never heard about it. If I'd known she was in some kind of danger, maybe I could have done something."

Joey sighed. "One more thing, I'd like you to agree to provide a DNA sample to help with the investigation into Holly's death," Joey said.

Randall waved his hand. "Fine. But what does me meeting her mother all those years ago have to do with her being killed?"

Joey shook his head and gazed at his notepad, and after a moment he looked up. "Mr. Madison, Holly was murdered right outside your daughter's home. And she thought maybe she was your daughter, too. Do you really have to ask what this has to do with you?"

CHAPTER 18

The limo skimmed silently over the George Washington Bridge into New York City, the five people inside quietly contemplating Joey's news. The mood since they'd left the house was subdued, but Randall had been trying to lighten it, reminiscing about the night when he'd met Cheryl Anderson.

"Daddy, please," Arlena sighed quietly.

"Look, kids." Randall became serious. "You know who I am. And I don't apologize for my life. I take responsibility for my actions."

Penelope was thankful she was sitting next to the door out of his direct line of sight. Sam sipped champagne from a flute, his arm draped over Arlena on the other side of her, and Max sat next to his dad across from them.

"But Daddy," Arlena said, exasperated. "Holly tried to reach out to you. Someone killed her and that same person might be after me. Don't you feel like we're partly to blame for what happened to her?"

Randall sighed and sat back against the leather seat, crossing an ankle over his knee. He put his arm around Max's shoulders, who stared out the window at the Hudson River. "If anyone decides to come after any of my kids, they're going to have to go through me first," he declared. "I still have some connections from the neighborhood. If this Detective Baglioni can't take care of it, I will."

Arlena sighed and looked at Sam.

"I love you kids. You know that," Randall said.

"We love you too, Dad," Max said quietly.

Père was a small French restaurant that Randall frequented in Midtown. Though it had been around for many years, it was still destination dining, unique in that it was popular with both tourists and native New Yorkers. Penelope had seen Père mentioned more than once on Page Six accompanied by blurry pictures of celebrities coming and going. She was more interested in sampling their menu, which had a reputation as innovative and fresh, and always evolving based on the season.

The restaurant was dimly lit and all of the tables were full. The low murmur of conversation paused momentarily as Randall Madison and his party were greeted at the door and escorted immediately to a table in the main room next to the bar. It normally took a few months to get a reservation for eight o'clock on a Saturday night at Père, but Randall had managed it with one phone call that afternoon. Penelope admired the eclectic mix of mismatched dishware and glasses on the white tablecloths, which gave the impression of being in someone's home rather than an upscale eatery. Adding to the warmth of the room was an open fireplace in a stone hearth that ran along the back wall and the smell of freshly baked bread in the air.

A young waitress in a long white apron appeared at their table as they settled into their seats. Randall ordered a round of dirty martinis to which she nodded pertly and strode over to the bar, her hands clasped behind her back. Penelope noticed that none of the wait staff was writing anything down, most likely trained to memorize their table orders. When their waitress returned with drinks, Randall grabbed one off of her tray and said, "Best martini in town."

As they drank their cocktails some of the tension from the limo began to ease. The couple at the next table stole a couple of glances at Arlena and Sam, who were sitting close together and discretely linking fingers under the table.

The waitress quietly reappeared at the table along with a well-dressed, compact older gentleman. "So nice to see you again, Randall," he said, patting Randall on the back.

"Louie!" Randall said. "You're looking fit."

"Not as fit as you," Louie said, crinkles forming around his eyes. "Do you have in mind what you'd like this evening?"

"Bring us *Marche du Chef*," Randall said. He glanced at Arlena and added, "But no shellfish."

Penelope searched her culinary school memories for the phrase and remembered it roughly translated into "Chef's Choice."

"And we'll have another round of these." He tilted his empty martini glass towards the waitress.

"Absolutely. I think you'll be pleased with what we have tonight," Louie said, bowing slightly to the group. "Off you go, Brigitte." Louie shooed the waitress towards the bar and headed off to the kitchen.

"Daddy always knows where to go and what to order," Arlena said, rubbing her father's shoulder, letting the last of her frustration towards him fall away. He leaned back and grasped her hand.

Brigitte returned with five martini glasses, each filled to the brim with what looked and tasted like liquid silver. Penelope planned to savor this experience and carry it forward to inspire her own food. She took in her surroundings and thought about her dinner companions, realizing that even though Max and

Arlena had grown up separately and away from their father, when they were all together they acted like a very traditional family.

Max draped his arm across the back of Penelope's chair. "You look beautiful tonight," he said, his fingers tapping lightly on her shoulder.

"Thanks, Max," she said. She picked up her martini from the table, being careful not to spill any of it, and took a sip. Max continued to gaze at her, taking his own drink in his hand.

Just then Brigitte reappeared at their table, balancing a tray of beautifully arranged dishes. The group fell silent and watched as she placed the plates in the middle of the table. "Please enjoy our baked *Camembert, Boeuf Bourguignonne, Blanquette de Veau, Piperade*, and the chef's special *Cassoulet*."

Louie, who had been overseeing from a distance, walked over and poured red wine into their long-stemmed glasses. "A gift from the chef," he said, showing the label to Randall. "We do hope you enjoy." Louie and Brigitte made a quick exit and Randall began passing around the plates, marveling at the way everything looked and smelled.

After they'd finished dessert, a selection of *pots de crème*, Penelope excused and headed to the ladies' room.

"I'll join you," Arlena said.

They entered the restaurant's bathroom and stood next to each other at the mirror.

"Everything was perfect. I wouldn't mind having that *Cassoulet* at home," Arlena hinted, eyeing her lipstick in the mirror.

"I'll have to come up with my own version, Penelope said. "I never knew your dad was so funny." She turned towards the line of stalls along the wall and entered the closest one.

"Daddy loves making people laugh," Arlena said distractedly. She rubbed her hands down her flat stomach. "That was a nice splurge but I have to take it easy now. I can't look like I gained weight from one day to the next." Penelope emerged and washed her hands at the sink.

The toilet in the far corner of the room flushed and Penelope glanced at Arlena. Brigitte emerged from the stall, tucking a stray strand of hair back into the rubber band of her ponytail with one hand and her phone into her apron pocket with the other. She looked at the floor as she approached the sinks to wash her hands.

"I'm sorry, please excuse me," Brigitte said, blushing as she lathered her hands at the far end of the counter.

"No need to be sorry," Arlena said. "Thanks for taking care of us tonight."

The limo slipped around the corner of the restaurant right as they stepped outside. They were bundled up in coats and scarves and stood close together to ward off the cold.

"Oh perfect," Randall said, nodding at a group of paparazzi standing on the opposite corner. Some of them began to move across the street towards the entrance of the restaurant.

"Hey Sam! Sam, over here!" one of them shouted as camera flashes lit up the night. Sam took a step closer to Arlena, turning towards her and shielding her from the approaching crowd. Randall lit a cigarette and raised his arms wide in a "come and get me" gesture.

Penelope, who stood in the middle of the group, took a step behind Max, his tall frame big enough to shield her for the most part. There were probably twenty photographers, all of them yelling and flashing bulbs at them, closing in on them from both sides of the sidewalk. She couldn't make out any of their faces through the flashes. They all looked alike in their puffy coats and knit hats pulled low against the cold.

A few passing cars slowed to take a look at the paparazzi, their heads swiveling from the crowd to the limo to see who they were targeting. Horns blared and a police siren sounded, and Penelope could hear the jackhammer of a road crew somewhere nearby. She was amazed at how loud the street was compared to the peaceful interior of the restaurant they'd just left.

The limo eased up to the curb in front of them and the driver jumped out to help them inside. The shouting from the photographers became more intense as Sam and Arlena made their move to leave. More horns blared from the blocked traffic and a backfire boomed down the street. Randall waved the driver back inside the limo, opening the passenger door himself and ushering the others into the relative quiet inside. When they were all inside, he stood up and waved one last time at the shouting group of photographers. "That's it, fellas. Show's over. Go get warm."

"Thanks, Randall. Who are you married to now?" one of the photographers shouted back.

"You'll have to figure that one out for yourself, buddy," Randall said, smiling widely at the group. Flashes lit up the side of the black limo like lightning in the dark night. Randall climbed inside and slammed the door, tapping on the glass separating the driver compartment from the passenger area to signal to the driver to go.

One of the photographers darted around the limo and knocked on the window right next to Penelope's head. She shrunk away as he flashed his camera through the dark tinted windows. She was grateful when the limo slid forward into traffic.

"Can you believe these guys?" Randall said. He lowered the separation glass. "Come on, get us out of here."

The driver nodded and stepped on the gas, then slammed on the brakes suddenly to avoid hitting a photographer who stood in front of the car snapping pictures through the windshield.

They were like a swarm of bees descending on the car, the frantic shouts and sounds of snapping cameras muffled through the thick glass. Penelope shifted closer to Max and away from the window, shielding her eyes from the flashing bulbs at the mob of people surrounding the car.

"Go!" Randall shouted.

The driver floored the gas pedal and the limo jerked forward and to the left, brushing the legs of the photographer in front of them.

"Watch it, asshole," the man yelled, slapping his hand on Penelope's window as they passed, leaving a greasy palm print.

Penelope caught a glimpse of a tattoo snaking out from under the photographer's sleeve. As they raced away, she glanced back at the photographers who had spilled out onto the street, still snapping pictures of the limo, risking getting hit by oncoming traffic. She watched the headlights of the cars dodging them from behind, blaring their horns as they passed, and wondered how much a picture of Arlena and Sam together was worth. Apparently it was enough for them to risk bodily injury.

Penelope leaned back on the seat, relieved they were on their way, another anonymous black limo in New York City.

"You okay?" Max asked her, grasping her hand loosely in his.

"Wow," Penelope said, laughing a bit. "I was holding my breath back there."

Max chuckled. "You get the full treatment around Sam, I guess. And Dad. They're always after Dad."

Penelope glanced across the way to Sam and Arlena, who

were turned towards each other, deep in conversation. Randall was next to them but engrossed in something on his phone, the screen lighting his face.

"I suppose one day they'll be coming for me," Max said. "And it will be for the things I'm doing, not only because of my family."

Penelope turned and looked him in the eyes. "Do you want that?"

"Maybe not the constant harassment, but yeah, I want to get to that level. This is my chosen career. I want the kind of success that attracts their attention."

"I hope you get what you want," Penelope said, squeezing his hand back. She flipped open the panel of the cooler that ran along the wall of the limo. It was stocked with bottled water, beer and in another compartment, bottles of wine. She grabbed a bottle of water and a napkin to wipe off the condensation, offering one to Max. He shook his head, selecting a bottle of wine instead. Penelope sighed as he waved it at her in an inviting gesture. Rolling her eyes, she picked up the wine key next to the napkins and handed it to him.

"Not the whole bottle," she said.

"Of course not," he said, reaching behind her and pulling two wine glasses from the rack next to the cooler.

CHAPTER 19

Penelope finished her first cup of coffee during the drive to Glendale High School the next morning, which sat right outside of the center of town. She zipped her car keys in the pocket of her thin Lycra jacket and breathed in the crisp air as she made her way from the parking lot to the football field. There was a quarter-mile track surrounding the field and Penelope planned to sprint for two miles. Some days she liked to run as fast as she could, feeling her heart pumping through the effort. It always relieved her stress.

Penelope started off at a jog, warming up her cold legs and arms so they would work harder for her in a few minutes. After the second turn around the rust-colored rubber track, she picked up her pace, leaning forward into the wind, her arms slicing the air at her sides. By the time she was on her second mile, she ran in a full out effort, her breath puffing in and out like a locomotive steaming along a track.

Penelope slowed to a jog and decided on one more lap around to cool down. She glanced at her watch and was pleased she'd finished at a respectable pace. Making her final turn, a flash of movement in the football stadium seats caught her attention. She shaded her eyes and looked up, slowing to a walk. Flags attached to the railings fluttered in the breeze, flashing the school colors of red and white. Penelope walked quickly around the final turn and to the gate that led out to the parking lot.

Back inside her warm car, Penelope took a sip of tepid coffee. She ducked her head and looked up at the stadium seats through the windshield, jumping when she saw someone standing in the top row staring down at her car. The person was wearing a hooded sweatshirt and the sun was at their back, making it impossible for Penelope to see their face.

Her heart skipped a beat and she started the car, popping the locks down quickly as she eased out of the parking space. As she turned and drove towards the exit, she looked at the person in the bleachers and felt they were still watching her, turning to follow her car's progress from the lot. She rolled through the stop sign at the lot's entrance and exited quickly back onto the main road.

A few minutes later Penelope turned into the parking lot of Glendale Grocery a few miles down the road from the school. She parked and nervously glanced around, relieved that no one else was in the parking lot.

"Good morning," an elderly woman greeted her right inside the store as the automatic door slid open. It was early still and the morning smells of coffee, donuts and pastries from the bakery filled the air.

The woman handed her a colorful sales flyer with the day's specials and a voucher for a cup of coffee. "You're one of the first customers today, so the coffee is on us," she said proudly, soft white hair floating around her head. She began gathering up another flyer and coupon for another customer entering behind Penelope.

Penelope picked up a hand basket and made her way through the store, selecting items from the produce section. She then strolled to the bakery to claim her free coffee and get some bagels, pointing at her choices through the thick glass. "Black, no sugar," she said, handing him the coffee voucher.

The deli worker passed a bag of bagels and croissants over the counter to her and placed a large cup of coffee on top of the case.

"Thank you," Penelope said, tucking the bag into her basket. After picking up some cream cheese and half and half from the dairy aisle, she wandered to the registers and stood in a short line, her coffee in one hand, her shopping basket dangling from the other.

Penelope raised her coffee cup to her lips and glanced at the magazine rack on her right as she waited, reading the tabloid headlines: "Meryl Streep Has Alien Baby," "How Kim Kardashian lost 80 lbs!" and "Bad Bikini Bodies." Penelope rolled her eyes and shifted her weight, shaking her head at the exploitative pictures of unsuspecting celebrities looking less than fabulous. She looked to the right side of the aisle. "Plastic Surgery Gone Wrong!" yelled from another headline.

"Oh no," Penelope whispered under her breath. Underneath the large bold type was a picture of Arlena, her face and lips swollen behind big black sunglasses and a thin grey hooded jacket pulled up over her hair. She was tugging the hood as close to her face as possible but it did little to hide her identity or her severe allergic reaction.

Penelope placed her shopping basket on the ground between her feet and plucked the magazine from the rack. Tucking the paper coffee cup awkwardly in the crook of her arm, she flipped through the pages, looking for the article inside. Finding it on page nine, she skimmed it quickly.

Horror queen Arlena Madison has gone under the knife with disastrous results. The budding beauty and daughter of Randall Madison was photographed rushing from her doctor's office, trying in vain to hide from our cameras. All we can say is...thanks, Arlena. Now we don't even have to watch your movies to be truly scared...

"Excuse me, miss?" The cashier beckoned from her perch behind the register. Penelope glanced up, alarmed, her thoughts lost in the article. She looked behind her and saw two impatient looking women giving her dirty looks from behind their full shopping carts.

"Oh, sorry, go ahead." Penelope knelt down and picked up her basket, moving out of line to let the other customers go ahead of her. She stepped back and glanced down the row of registers, each of them anchored by magazine racks, all of them full of the edition she held in her hand. Penelope's heart sank and she got back in line, contemplating how she would tell Arlena this latest bit of bad news.

"Are they serious?" Arlena said, snatching the magazine from Penelope's hand. Everyone was gathered in the kitchen except for Max, who was sleeping in and would miss the newest drama unfolding in Arlena's life. Arlena tore through the pages until she found the article, her eyes widening as she read the outright lies on the page.

"Everyone will see you back at work tomorrow looking like yourself." Sam eased the magazine from her hands. He placed it on the counter and hugged Arlena. She hugged him back and nodded stiffly, but picked the tabloid up again when he let her go, holding it closer and staring at the pictures.

"Those jerks," she said softly.

"I'm sorry, Arlena. I wanted to show you before someone else did."

"I know," Arlena said, flinging the magazine back down on the counter.

Randall fumed at the other end of the island while Penelope began unloading the groceries, quietly placing items on the far counter next to the stove.

"I should sue them." Arlena sat at a stool next to Sam.

"Everyone knows these kinds of papers are full of lies. If you sue them, you might bring more attention to it than they'd get if you just left it alone." Sam rubbed Arlena's back as she propped her chin on her fist, her elbow on the counter. "I've been through this before. It's not worth the trouble."

"How did they get that picture of you?" Penelope asked over her shoulder. "You went straight home from the set, right?"

"Yep. This was taken before we left. I can see the corner of my trailer," Arlena said, pointing to the edge of the picture.

"Do you think it was one of the crew?" Penelope asked.

"It happens," Sam said. "Someone on my last set took pictures of me in my trailer through a crack in the door. Everyone has a camera on their phone now, it's easy."

"Daddy," Arlena said, "what should I do?"

"Screw them," Randall grumbled. He stood and walked over to Penelope, taking a bagel from the deli bag. "Like Sam says, don't give them the satisfaction. Focus on your work. That's the best advice I can give."

CHAPTER 20

Sal Marco lived on Elm Street in the older section of South Point in the house where he'd grown up. The streets were lined with old elm trees and regal homes that sat close to the road. Warm lights lit the two-story brick house and shadows of party guests moved across the windows.

Sam and Arlena walked hand in hand to the house while Penelope followed with Randall at her side. They rang the bell, hearing faint conversation on the other side of the front door before it opened.

A smiling Sal opened the door. "There they are, my main man and my leading lady." Sal reached out his arms in a greeting gesture, bringing Arlena in for a hug and a kiss on the cheek and then patting Sam's arm roughly. Sam placed his hand on the small of Arlena's back and ushered her inside.

Sal watched them pass then stepped onto the porch to give Randall a gruff hug. "So good to see you, my old friend."

"It's been a while, Salvatore," Randall said, pulling out of the hug and holding Sal at arm's length. The two men turned to go inside, Randall's arm draped heavily over Sal's shoulders.

Sal stopped short, remembering Penelope on the porch. "Come in, Chef, so glad you could join us." He motioned for her to go ahead of them.

"Thanks for inviting me." Penelope stepped into the long front hallway. It was lined with family photos, some of them vintage looking. Penelope recognized Sal as a child and a young man in many of them, with his parents and other family members at various ages. In the center of the hallway was an oversized wedding photo of Sal and Paige. It was surrounded by smaller pictures of them posing in exotic locales, mainly sandy beaches or icy mountaintops.

The hallway led to a large study at the back of the house, where most of the party attendees had gathered. Penelope walked over to the bar and stood next to Arlena and Sam.

"Would you like a drink?" Sam asked, motioning to a young bartender wearing a crisp white dress shirt.

"I'd love a Cosmo." Penelope realized she'd lost Sal and Randall somewhere along the way. Maybe they were reminiscing over the photographs in the hallway.

"Are you all right, Pen? You seem distracted," Arlena said, accepting a champagne cocktail from Sam.

"I wanted to talk to Sal about what happened on Friday." She accepted her pink martini from Sam.

"Don't stress about it," Arlena said. "He wouldn't have invited you over for dinner if there was still a problem."

"Unless he wants to let me down easy by firing me after drinks and a home-cooked meal," Penelope muttered.

The walls of the study were lined with built-in bookshelves that housed hundreds of books. Paintings hung around the edges of the room and the furniture was modern but retro in style. "This is a cool house," Penelope said, admiring the shelf next to the bar.

"Daddy says Sal inherited it after his parents passed away. They've updated it, of course," Arlena said. She nodded towards the far end of the room. "Wow, is that a Mondrian?"

"I don't know much about art. But I think so." Penelope

swept her gaze around the room, making a mental note to Google Mondrian when she got home. Maybe she could ask Joey about him too.

"...and then we couldn't get the same horse for the shoot, so we had to redo all of the horse scenes with a horse who could stand to work with Bobby," Sal's voiced boomed from the doorway of the study. He entered with Randall, both of them laughing. Everyone turned and some started laughing along with them, although they hadn't heard the whole story. Penelope wondered which Bobby they were talking about. De Niro? Redford?

Penelope took that moment to pull Sal aside. "Sal, I have to tell you," she said in a low voice, "the thing with Arlena...it turns out it wasn't the lemons, it was something with her makeup."

"Randall was telling me on the way in. Let's talk about it later, huh?" Sal said, patting her shoulder and turning back to the others. Turning to Arlena he said, "I'm glad you're feeling better. Let me tell you, I'm going to find out who messed with your things and they're going to be sorry."

Arlena glanced away, not sure how to respond.

Changing the subject, Sal said, "Hey, you probably don't remember this, but Randall brought you here when you maybe two or three years old. I could see then you were something special. And I was right."

"Thanks, Sal. Daddy never mentioned that."

"It was a long time ago. I don't have any kids of my own, but I've watched all of his grow up nicely from afar. Hey, Randall," Sal shouted across the room. "You never told Arlena about bringing her here when she was a baby?"

"You've got a better memory than me from those days, Sal," Randall shouted back at his friend.

"I guess that's true," Sal said, shaking his head. "Tonight I want you to enjoy yourselves. But we're running behind schedule, and I expect you all to stay sharp for the next two weeks so we can get this little gem in the can."

They all agreed, nodding and promising to do their best.

"I feel better now." Sal winked at the trio. "Excuse me. I have to check on the kitchen. My wife gets lost back there."

A burst of laughter erupted from the group of people surrounding Randall, who said, "And that was only the first time. You can imagine how she felt after the fifth." He slapped one of the men on the back and motioned with his empty beer bottle towards the bar, excusing himself.

"Daddy's having a good time," Arlena said as Randall sauntered over to them. A pretty redhead got up from one of the chairs and followed him, taking the spot beside him at the bar and smiling widely at him.

Arlena tapped her father on the shoulder and whispered under her breath, "Daddy, she's an actress in the movie. Don't get too familiar with her for my sake, at least while we're still working together."

Randall waved Arlena off and turned to talk to the shapely read head. Arlena rolled her eyes at Penelope, who looked away. Everyone fell into different conversations, which all began to fade and run together for Penelope as watched the other guests chatting in loose groups throughout the room. There were about twenty people in the study, Penelope recognizing everyone as either an actor or writer. She was the only member of the set crew at the party.

Just then Paige stepped up to the bar and said, "Charles, another Manhattan, please."

"Yes, ma'am," the bartender said, grabbing a cocktail shaker and getting to work on her drink. She said to Penelope, "I'm so glad you're here. I asked Sal to invite you because I wanted to ask you a favor."

"Oh sure," Penelope said. "What can I do?"

"It's about the wrap party. Sal wants to do it here at the house, and I was hoping your team could handle it. We can discuss specifics later, but I wanted you to see the kitchen and the house and get a feel for the place."

"Sure. We'll do something nice. It will be easy."

"That's a relief. We're off to Tuscany right after Sal's done here and we're sending the staff ahead of us, including our chef. We'll be there six months for his next project, and I'm trying to coordinating everything. It's becoming overwhelming. If you could handle the wrap party that's one less thing on my plate." Paige turned to Arlena. "I've been hearing wonderful things about the movie. I wish I could get over to the set every day and watch you work. Sal's been considering this one for a long time."

"Oh yeah?" Arlena asked.

"I gave him the book over fifteen years ago, back when we first started dating. It took him this long to develop it and find space on his calendar. You know how busy we all get. Something bigger was always coming along and *Remember the Fall* kept getting pushed to the side."

Charles set Paige's drink in front of her and she picked it up to take a sip. "If you ask your dad," she motioned at Randall, "he'll tell you this room hasn't changed much at all since Sal got his start in movies. Of course, I was still in grade school..."

"It's exactly like I remember it," Randall said.

"Sal's got a long tradition of having the cast over for Sunday dinner. You guys work such long days, sometimes I feel like I don't see Sal at all," Paige said. Her severe blond bangs snagged her long eyelashes when she blinked, causing them to bounce on her forehead. Penelope fought the urge to reach up and brush them from her eyes. Paige's collar bones stood out sharply above the neckline of her shimmery silver top and she wore skintight black jeans with silver flats. Even in flat shoes she stood a few inches taller than Arlena.

"I know what you mean," Randall said. "Movies are murder on relationships. But you guys have been together a long time."

"Together fifteen years, married for twelve," Paige said. "We met on *Haymaker*, my first movie." She took another sip of her drink. "And my last, it turned out." She glanced around the room at the other guests. "A show business marriage of fifteen years is like fifty years for a regular marriage, isn't it?"

Her guests all chuckled politely at her joke.

"Everyone knows I wasn't the first Mrs. Marco," she continued, glancing at Arlena. "But I've lasted the longest." Paige patted Randall's arm and said, "Please excuse me, we're about to sit down and I need to check on the kitchen." She headed towards the hallway, saying a brief hello to another guest leaning on the bookcase by the door.

"Paige is wonderful," Randall said, in an uncharacteristically lowered voice. "She saves Sal from himself, keeps him sane. I knew his first two wives and let's just say the third time's the charm. For Sal anyway."

"All right, everyone." Paige appeared once again in the doorway of the library and swept her arms towards the dining room. "Dinner is served."

The dining room walls were covered in dark red silk. Antique wall sconces that had been painted white were spaced evenly around the room, large white pillar candles burning on each one. A matching chandelier hung over the center of the long wooden table that was covered in colorfully patterned dishes and sparkling stemware.

"Looks beautiful, dear," Sal said, kissing Paige on her cheek.

Paige thanked him, placing her cocktail at the head seat at the end of the table as she watched her guests take their seats.

"We're dining family style tonight, so everyone dig in when you get settled," she said over the murmured conversation in the room.

Penelope took the empty seat next to her, the legs of her chair scraping the wooden floor as she pulled it from the table. Two bottles of wine made their way around the table, passed from guest to guest in opposite directions as Charles came through the swinging kitchen door with the appetizer course, two large platters piled high with antipasto, a varied selection of cheeses, meats and olives.

"Let's all take a moment here," Sal said when he saw that everyone had found a seat. He looked at Paige at the opposite end and bowed his head. He grasped hands with Randall and Arlena, who flanked him and said, "Let us give thanks for this bountiful meal, for each other's company and for our health on this beautiful day. We are lucky to be together and for this we are eternally grateful. Amen." He looked up again. "Let's eat."

After a few minutes Charles reappeared with a large bowl of salad and cleared away the picked over platters of antipasto. He returned quickly with two tureens filed with the main pasta course, penne ala vodka, and everyone began passing them around the table.

"It's been a rough first week, huh?" Randall said quietly to Sal after he'd served himself some pasta.

Sal cut his eyes at him, a flash of annoyance darkening his brow. "You said that right." He stabbed at his plate, piercing a cluster of penne. He pointed it at Randall. "If I didn't know any better, I'd say someone was trying to get back at me for something."

Randall grimaced. "You're the hometown hero around here, the famous director who never forgot his roots. Who do you think is trying to get back at you, and for what? I think it's my family they're after, either me or Arlena. Or both."

Sal forked the pasta into his mouth and glanced down the table. "Who knows." He took a quick look at Arlena, who was engrossed in a conversation with Sam. "Maybe we're being paranoid and what's happening on set is just bad luck."

"That girl getting killed outside Arlena's house was no coincidence," Randall said darkly. Sal put his fork down and said a quick prayer under his breath. Randall paused a moment then said, "You and I have been around long enough to have rubbed a lot of people the wrong way. If it is you they're after, why now? Has anything happened lately?"

Sal shook his head, gazing at a spot over Randall's shoulder. "Like you said, we're in my hometown, but I've never made a movie here. Maybe someone thinks it should have stayed that way."

"So, what, you ticked off the prom king back in high school and now he's out for revenge?" Randall chuckled. "You're not hurting anyone by working here. Actually you're creating jobs and bringing money in."

"I don't know," Sal said, a note of resignation in his voice. "Sometimes you think you're doing the best you can for people and then it turns out you're doing the worst thing possible."

Paige picked at her pasta from the other end of the table and watched them talk, straining to hear their conversation. The kitchen door whooshed open and Charles appeared with two long bread baskets that he set quickly down on the table.

"Charles," Paige said, waving him over.

He hurried over and knelt down next to her while she whispered something to him from behind her napkin. He nodded quickly and he stood up, disappearing back into the kitchen.

Paige set her fork down and picked up her wine glass, leaning back against her chair. "What did you think of dinner?" she asked Penelope, her gaze a bit unfocused.

Penelope swallowed a piece of bread and nodded. "Excellent."

"Ready for dessert?" she asked, eyeing the other plates around her.

"Sure," Penelope said, noticing that many of the guests were still eating, talking and laughing together.

"Good, you're going to like it," Paige said, gazing at the kitchen door.

When they'd finished dessert, chocolate covered cannolis with sliced almonds accompanied by espresso, Sal invited the actors and writers to the study to discuss the week ahead. Penelope decided to take a look at the kitchen and meet the Marco's chef while she waited.

The kitchen was small compared to most modern houses, but it had bright white cabinets and stainless steel appliances, which made it feel like a larger space. Charles was at the sink washing dishes, and the chef, a large man with graying hair, stood at the island drying his knives.

"Can I help you?" the chef asked as Penelope entered.

"Hi, I'm Penelope Sutherland...I'm with the movie crew." She hooked her thumb over towards the door in the general direction of the study. "Paige asked me to do the wrap party here and I thought I'd take a look at the kitchen."

"She did mention something about that," he said flatly, looking back down at his knives.

Charles glanced over his shoulder at her, his sleeves pushed up on his forearms above sink. Penelope eyed the space, visualizing where she would set up her crew's stations to prep for the party. She went to the kitchen door and looked out through the windows at the backyard. A two-story barn-like structure sat at the edge of the property.

"What's that building used for?" Penelope asked the chef.

He sighed. "That's Mr. Marco's home office and studio. They've used it for parties like the one you'll be doing. Mrs. Marco should have mentioned that to you."

"Is it heated?" Penelope asked, still looking at the building about fifty yards from the house.

The chef paused from his polishing and glanced up at her. "Of course it is. He works out there." He shook his head and began slipping his knives into the different sized slots of his canvas knife roll.

"Oh, right. You said that," Penelope said. She hesitated, thinking twice about bothering him again, then said, "Is there anything I should know about how the kitchen works?"

The chef rolled up the knife holder and said, "That behind you," he flicked his eyes over her left shoulder, "is called a refrigerator. We keep things in there that will spoil if they get too warm. And this," he glanced behind him, "is an oven. That's where we heat things up, or cook, as it's sometimes called."

Penelope crossed her arms and willed the redness out of her face. "Gee thanks, that's very helpful."

"I hope you have a wonderful party. I'm sure it will be amazing," he said, sarcasm rolling off his tongue effortlessly. He slid open a drawer on the island and tucked the knives inside.

Charles snuck a glance at Penelope over his shoulder and when he saw the chef wasn't looking he pulled a face and rolled his eyes. Penelope hid a smile behind her hand.

The chef pulled on his jacket and exited the kitchen door, sticking a cigarette from his coat pocket in the corner of his mouth. Penelope watched his back as he slipped around the side of the house towards the street. Looking again towards the old barn, she saw Paige emerge from the door and light a cigarette, blowing out a large cloud of smoke. She shivered and pulled the collar of her long wool coat closer around her neck.

Charles washed the last pot and turned off the water. Drying his hands on a white towel he said, "Don't mind him. He's like that with everyone, especially other chefs."

"Unfortunately I know the type," Penelope said.

"You want to take a look at the building?" Charles asked, rolling his sleeves back down and buttoning them at the wrists.

"Sure," Penelope said, watching Paige out in the yard, leaning up against the barn. She pulled another cigarette out of her coat pocket and lit it using the end of the one still burning.

"Grab your coat."

Penelope retrieved her coat and they stepped outside, the cold air bit at Penelope's warm cheeks. "Hi, Paige," she said as they approached. "I wanted to look at the barn."

"Help yourself," Paige slurred, motioning unsteadily at the building behind her.

"Are you okay?" Penelope asked, alarmed that Paige suddenly seemed tipsy when she'd seemed relatively sober at dinner.

"Perfect. Take your time," she said, and weaved back towards the kitchen door.

After she'd gone, Charles said, "She'll be fine, I'll make sure. Don't worry."

They entered the barn and Charles flipped a wall switch, illuminating dozens of antique lanterns strung with wire across the ceiling. "This building was originally built in the early 1800s. Mr. Marco spent a small fortune to have it moved here in pieces and reassembled on the property." Charles nodded at a ladder staircase against the back wall. "His home studio is upstairs, where he writes and edits the movies. Down here is open space, mostly used for rehearsals or sometimes a local production. It's pretty big so you can arrange whatever floor plan you want."

Penelope nodded and walked the space, pulling her scarf tighter around her neck.

Charles noticed and said, "I'll kick the heat on a few hours before, and if it snows I'll clear a path to the house. And I can get the tables and chairs set up, serve, tend bar, whatever." He turned and led her back to the door.

When Penelope and Charles reentered the kitchen they saw Paige standing at the island, still in her wool coat, pouring herself a glass of wine. "You guys...um...guys find what you needed to find out there?" Paige asked, sloshing some wine onto the counter.

"I think so," Penelope said.

Charles hung his jacket back on the hook and walked quickly to the island, using a dishtowel to wipe the wine from the counter.

"They've finished up their meeting. I think they're waiting for you." Paige motioned with her wineglass towards the dining room and study beyond.

"Thanks," Penelope said. "I'll touch base with you soon to talk about menu ideas."

"Penelope." Paige stared at her and spoke deliberately, as if practicing a foreign language. She paused for an uncomfortably long moment then said, "I wanted to tell you...that what...whatever you decide is fine." She paused and pulled in a sharp breath, pressing the back of one bony had against her mouth. "We're going to be out of the country the very next day. Off to Tuscany." Paige drifted towards the kitchen door, pulling her cigarettes from her coat pocket and fumbling with the knob for a few seconds before she was outside again.

Penelope watched her go then looked at Charles, who was leaning against the sink. He sighed and shrugged his shoulders. "Call me if you think of anything else you might need," he said quietly, grabbing his coat from the hook and following Paige out into the night.

CHAPTER 21

Penelope skidded out of the driveway the next morning, rolling through a puddle of slush at the end of the driveway. Her travel coffee mug tilted dangerously in the cup holder as she took the turn and she grabbed it with one gloved hand, righting it as she sped out onto the street. When she got to the next corner, she took a hard right and her messenger bag spilled onto the floor, all of her belongings sliding out onto the floor mat.

"Crap."

She had dashed out of the house twenty minutes earlier without her phone. She made it halfway to the set before realizing she'd forgotten it and had to turn back. Now she had to hustle to get to work before her team did.

The sun wouldn't be up for a couple of hours. Penelope didn't see any other cars on the road as she waited at the red light in the town square of Glendale. She glanced at the digital clock on her dashboard and the green numbers glared dully back at her: 3:56 a.m. The cast and crew would be in at five, and she always liked to be in an hour before them to prep for the day.

"Come on..." she mumbled at the red light dangling over the intersection.

She was beginning to think the traffic light was stuck in the red position when it suddenly changed over to green. Penelope gave it gas and hurried out of town to hook up with the parkway. South Point was only one exit away so if she moved quickly she might only be ten or fifteen minutes behind schedule.

As she sped towards the access road, the alarm on her phone pierced the quiet interior of the car, notifying her that it was her start time on set and she was officially late for work. She glanced down and saw her phone was lying on the passenger side floor with the rest of the contents of her bag, flipped up against the door. The foghorn alarm bleated loudly and she wondered why she had chosen the most annoying ring tone she could possibly find.

Penelope reached down and tried to grab the phone with her right hand, still gripping the steering wheel with her left. Keeping her eyes on the deserted road ahead, she lunged in her seat to grab it, but her fingers only swiped the air in front of it. She didn't think she could stand listening to her annoying alarm the whole way to work and maintain her sanity, so she decided to slow down so she could reach the phone. Penelope thought about pulling over, but she was on a two lane access road with guardrails on either side and there was no safe place to do it.

After another few seconds she decided to go for it. She checked her mirrors and saw no one approaching from either direction. She slowed to a crawl and then stopped. She put her truck in park, undid her seat belt and leaned over to grab her phone. Penelope yanked off her glove in her teeth and punched the flashing OFF button on the screen to silence the alarm.

Sighing in relief, she tossed her phone onto the passenger seat and grabbed the seat belt from behind her shoulder, pulling it back into place. She took a sip of coffee and put the truck back in gear. Right as she was about to hit the gas, red and blue lights lit up her back window. Penelope's eyes jerked to the rearview mirror.

"Are you kidding me right now?" Penelope whispered harshly. She put the car back into park and stared at the flashing lights.

A sharp rap on her driver's side window startled her and she jumped in her seat. Penelope turned and saw the back of a police officer's gloved hand rapping on her window and a flashlight beam shining around the interior of her car. She pressed the button to lower the window.

"License and registration, please."

Penelope leaned over and rummaged through her glove box, pulling the plastic envelope that contained her title and insurance documents from beneath a wad of Starbucks napkins. She snatched her wallet off the floor of the car, which was hidden under her notebook and a bunch of scattered invoices, and pulled out her driver's license.

"How are we doing today, ma'am?" The officer was still shining the flashlight around the car but Penelope could tell it was a woman's voice.

"I'm fine, Officer. Is there a problem?"

"Where are you headed?"

"To work. I'm running late actually..."

"Did you realize you were stopped in an active thruway, ma'am?"

"Oh yes. I dropped my phone."

"We have a law against talking or texting while driving in this state," the officer responded easily, cutting her off.

"I know. I wasn't texting. The phone fell on the floor and the alarm was going off, so I—"

"Have you been drinking this evening?" the officer interrupted.

"No. I'm on my way to work."

"At four in the morning?"

"I work on a movie set. Plus, I would never drink—"

"Step out of the car, please," the officer said.

"Really?"

"Step out of the car."

Penelope reluctantly clicked off her seat belt and opened the door, stepping out into the cold. When she came face to face with the policewoman she recognized her immediately.

"Hey, you're—"

"I'm going to ask you to perform a field sobriety test. Please step this way," Officer Jenkins said, motioning with her flashlight as she walked towards her patrol car.

"Honestly, I haven't been drinking. I swear, I'm on my way to work," Penelope said again. They were in a deserted area of the access road, sandwiched between a rusty guardrail and a thick section of trees separating them from the parkway. A few cars whisked past on the other side of the trees but they were otherwise alone.

"Then this should be easy for you," Officer Jenkins said tightly. Her lips were set in a straight line on her deeply tanned face and the parentheses around it were dug in deep. She crossed her arms over her chest and nodded at a spot on the pavement, the red and blue flashing lights lighting up the night around them. "Walk a straight line for me, heel to toe."

"Can I ask what makes you think I've been drinking?" Penelope asked, moving over to the area she indicated and heel-toeing her Doc Martins together on the asphalt.

"You stopped your vehicle in an active roadway, very dangerous. I observed you drinking something in your car. You were using your cell phone in direct violation of New Jersey state law, and you were driving erratically before you stopped. And you did not come to a complete stop at the stop sign on the corner of Randolph and Carter."

Penelope had taken ten or so steps but she stopped then and looked up at Officer Jenkins, who still stood with her arms crossed tightly at her chest. "Randolph and Carter...the intersection at the end of my street? You followed me all the way from my house?"

"Keep walking, Miss Sutherland. I wouldn't want to add 'failing to comply with a police officer's instructions' to the list." Officer Jenkins ducked her head and walked alongside Penelope, keeping her eyes on Penelope's feet.

After she had taken fifty steps, Officer Jenkins said, "Turn and face me, Miss Sutherland."

Penelope braced herself against the cold air and turned towards Officer Jenkins.

"Stand on one leg," she said.

Penelope stood for a moment and stared at her in disbelief. "Which leg, Officer?"

"Let's start with the right one," Officer Jenkins said, a smile cutting briefly across her thin lips.

Penelope sighed loudly and raised her left knee in the air, standing firmly and solidly on the pavement. She stared into the eyes of the other woman, not wavering in her gaze or her stance.

Officer Jenkins moved closer and stood a few inches from Penelope's face. She stared into her eyes a few more beats. "Please return to your vehicle while I check your license and registration."

Penelope fumed silently as she dropped her foot loudly on the pavement and turned towards her car. When she got in she turned up the heat and held her hands tightly against her mouth, blowing warm air into her gloves. She kept her eyes on the rearview mirror, watching Officer Jenkins' silhouette in the car behind her.

She seemed to be taking her time, sitting in the front seat of her cruiser and typing information into the keyboard attached to her dashboard. Penelope's eyes flicked to the digital clock in her car: 4:25. Her stomach did a flip when she realized she would be late for work for the first time since her movie catering career had begun. And right after she had determined not to get on Sal's bad side again.

Opening her cruiser's door slowly, Officer Jenkins got out and stretched before heading towards Penelope's car. Penelope watched her in the side view mirror until she was level with the window, then lowered the glass.

Officer Jenkins handed Penelope back her license and registration and a computer printed ticket attached to a yellow envelope. Penelope glanced at it and looked back out the window.

"I'm only going to cite you for impeding traffic on an active thruway and failing to stop at a stop sign. You passed the field sobriety test this morning," Officer Jenkins said, a tinge of disappointment in her voice. She rested her gloved hands on her thick leather belt.

"I passed because I don't typically drink on my way to work," Penelope said. She glanced back down at the ticket in her hand and saw the total at the bottom. Staring back at her in bold type: $350.

"You'll want to watch the drinking and driving. We're cracking down," Officer Jenkins said, leaning down to speak to Penelope directly through the window.

Penelope couldn't believe how badly her morning was going already. "Thanks, Officer," she said sharply, "for the warning."

Officer Jenkins patted the window frame. She stood up and walked back to her patrol car without another word.

Penelope watched her get into her cruiser and drive away, her car disappearing into the darkness ahead.

"Bitch," she whispered. "At least now I know where that awful pink lipstick came from."

CHAPTER 22

Penelope rushed all morning to catch up and she caught herself snapping orders at her team.

"Quentin, you need to move on those salads. We have no time today," she yelled to everyone in the prep tent.

Sensing her frustration, her crew worked quickly and quietly and mostly avoided her as much as they could. Penelope made a mental note to apologize to them after they got caught up.

The day moved quickly and by the end Penelope felt like she might survive after all. Sal had called an end to the day and they were busy getting everything put away when Penelope's phone buzzed in her back pocket. She walked towards the cab of her truck and pulled it out, glanced at the screen and saw Joey's name.

"Hello?" Even though she was stressed and exhausted, seeing his name on her phone lightened her mood. She climbed inside the cab of the truck and closed the door.

"Penelope, hi. It's Detective Baglioni."

"Joey," Penelope said, smiling. "What can I do for you?"

"I'm sorry to bother you at work. I know you're busy."

"It's fine. We're wrapping up for the day."

"I tried calling Arlena, but I kept getting her voicemail. Do you know if she's available?"

"Um, I haven't seen her for a while. They've been filming all day, so she might be resting or already on her way home. We're behind schedule because of the incidents on set last week. Sal's doubling up on some shoots until we catch up."

"I see..." he hesitated, seeming to weigh something.

"Or you could tell me whatever it is and I'll relay the message..."

He paused and Penelope wondered for a minute if she'd lost the connection with him.

"What are you doing later?" he finally asked.

"After finishing up here, I'm going home, eating dinner."

He paused again then said, "I wanted to tell Arlena, and Randall, actually, that I heard back from DIY-DNA. Holly did send them a kit and the results are surprising."

"Why? What did she find out?"

"It looks like she submitted her own DNA and that of her mother and her father, Cheryl and Bradley Anderson. She filled out the company's submission questionnaire and listed them as the second and third donors."

"Wait, she sent in the DNA of both of her parents?"

"That's weird, right? I assumed she was trying to figure out if Bradley Anderson was her dad. I didn't think about her mom at all. Anyway, the results came back and Dad's no match, and mom's a familial match," he said, sighing on the other end of the line.

Penelope stood up straighter. "Familial? What's that?"

"A familial match is a close relative, like a sibling maybe, or a cousin."

"Or maybe an aunt," Penelope said. "Remember when Randall said he recognized Cheryl's face but said her name was Rachel?"

"I do. And I checked. Cheryl has a twin sister named Rachel Harlow."

"So the Andersons aren't Holly's real parents? They're her aunt and uncle?"

"That's what I'm saying. Look, the Andersons are coming in within the hour. I'm letting you know because you helped me with this DNA company in the first place, and Arlena's told me more than once she doesn't mind me asking questions with you in the room."

"But wait...don't twins have the same DNA? How can they tell them apart?"

"They do if they're identical twins. But if they're fraternal it's different. I still have to confirm all of this but it might be why Holly ran off that night, finding out the truth about her parents might have set her off."

"Wow. I have to admit I wish you had happier news. It's been a rough day all around," Penelope sighed, crooking her phone on her shoulder and grabbing a stack of paper on the seat next to her to straighten into a pile.

"What do you mean? Did something else happen with Arlena or—"

"No, no, nothing like that," Penelope interrupted him, allowing some frustration to enter her voice. "I ran into your girlfriend. More like she ran into me, and gave me a $350 ticket on my way to work this morning."

"What do you mean *girlfriend*?" Joey asked in a sharp tone.

"Officer Jenkins? Your partner in...whatever," Penelope said, already regretting bringing up the topic.

Joey was speechless on the other end of the line and once again Penelope thought they had been cut off.

"Hello?" she said finally.

"Let me...first of all," he stammered. "Can you come by the station on your way home?"

"I don't know. I don't want to intrude on you two," Penelope said.

"Just come here. I need to talk to you," Joey said firmly.

CHAPTER 23

The police station sat right off of the parkway in a square brown building halfway between South Point and Glendale. The windows were tinted the same shade of brown, so the whole building looked like a thick block of chocolate.

Penelope pulled her Range Rover into a spot out front and walked through the automatic doors. The desk sergeant sat inside, gazing into a computer monitor and only looking up after Penelope had stood in front of him for a few seconds. He was an older man with a red face and a neck that drooped over his starched white collar.

"Help you?" he asked reluctantly.

"I'm here to see Detective Baglioni," Penelope responded.

"ID?"

Penelope dug through her messenger bag, eventually producing her wallet and extracting her license from inside.

He glanced at her ID for the briefest second then handed it back to her with a plastic visitor's pass, slapping a clipboard on the desk in front of her with a sign-in sheet attached to it. As she scratched her signature, he buzzed a door open to the left of the desk, gruffly directing her to follow the dingy green carpet all the way back to the Detective Squad.

She thanked him and proceeded through the doors, passing a row of glass enclosed offices on her left. She saw a few paperwork-strewn desks and one woman in a darkened office typing on a keyboard with her back to the door. Otherwise the station was very quiet, much to Penelope's surprise. She'd expected more activity, but then realized it was well past dinner time and maybe most of the people who worked there had already gone home.

At the end of the carpet Penelope came to a frosted glass door with "Detective Squad" painted on the glass. She saw Joey immediately after she pushed through the door.

Joey's face lit up when she entered. He was sitting at a desk, one of four pushed together in the otherwise empty room, his jacket draped over the back of one of the chairs.

"You made it," Joey said as he stood up and walked over to her. "Come on, let's go in here." He motioned to one of three interview rooms along the left wall. They entered and he shut the door behind them. "Thanks for coming down."

"Sure," Penelope said. She stood behind a table with four wooden chairs around it in the center of the room. "What did you want to talk about? Something about the case?"

"Look, I have to something to tell you about the case. But also, the thing with Nancy...Officer Jenkins—"

An intercom buzzed from the outer room and cut him off.

"Just a sec," he said, opening the door and walking back to his desk to pick up his desk phone.

"The Andersons are here," he said to her when he hung up. "I hate to ask, but can you hang out for a minute? I need to talk to you, but Holly's parents are here and I don't want to make them wait."

"I can for a bit. Wait, do they know about the DNA results?" she whispered, even though they were still alone in the squad room.

"No, not yet. Look, I won't be long. I want to clear something up with you. And I think I'd like you to hear what the Andersons have to say, if you're okay with that."

Penelope nodded tentatively. "Are you sure?"

"You helped the investigation more than once by providing new information, and you found Holly in the first place. It sounds crazy but whenever I talk to you, I feel like I get closer to the truth."

"What should I say if Holly's parents ask who I am?"

"Nothing. Stay in here and look busy," Joey said, grabbing a folder from the hanging file outside the door and handing it to her.

Before Penelope could answer, Joey said, "Take a seat. I'll be right outside." He went into the main room, being careful to leave the interview room door ajar. She looked down at the folder in her hand and flipped it open, seeing that it contained a collection of takeout menus.

Holly's parents came through to the squad room, looking very much like they did in the family photo she'd seen of them except now they appeared exhausted, their shoulders hunching forward as they greeted Joey. Cheryl's eyes were red and swollen, as if she'd recently been crying.

"Have a seat, please," Joey said, indicating the two chairs in front of his desk. "Thanks for coming in to speak with me."

Penelope watched them take their seats, Bradley throwing a quick look at her through the doorway before settling in his. Penelope flipped through her folder, pretending to study the paperwork inside. She felt uneasy about being there, but had to admit she really wanted to help Joey find out what had happened to Holly.

Mr. Anderson spoke first, his voice deep and shaky. "Have you found who killed our daughter?"

Joey cleared his throat. "Not yet, Mr. Anderson. We've been

tracking Holly's final days as you know, and we uncovered something that I need to ask you about."

"What is it?" Cheryl Anderson asked, her voice thick and scratchy.

"In the weeks before she died, was Holly acting differently? Did you notice anything out of the ordinary?"

"Um, no, I don't..." Cheryl stammered. "Everything was fine. I don't think so. We've already answered this question a hundred times."

"Holly withdrew $400 from her savings account," Bradley Anderson said suddenly. "I didn't tell you about it," he said, glancing at Cheryl. "When I got the account statement I asked her about it and she said it was for headshots. I told her that her savings account was for school and she needed permission to withdraw any money. We had already told her we'd help her with her auditioning expenses so it didn't make sense."

"Why didn't you tell me?" Cheryl asked.

Bradley looked down at his hands clenched together on the table. "The boys were both sick with the flu and you weren't feeling well yourself, remember? It wasn't a big deal, we decided we would put aside money for her for things like that...I handled it. She said she wouldn't do it again."

"That must be how she paid for this," Joey said. Penelope heard a shuffling of papers.

"What's DIY-DNA?" Cheryl asked.

"It's a private company that performs DNA tests," Joey said. "Holly sent samples off to them."

Cheryl gasped sharply. "What do you mean *samples*?" she asked, a bit indignantly.

"DNA samples from herself, and from Mr. Anderson," Joey said. "And from you, Mrs. Anderson."

"Me? What for?" she asked.

"Why do you think she did?" Joey asked gently.

Penelope heard heavy silence and then the sniffling of tears.

"Because she guessed that we weren't her parents," Bradley said in a hoarse whisper.

"What are you saying, Mr. Anderson?" Joey prodded.

"I mean, we're not her parents." Bradley's voice grew louder and firmer. "She was suspicious. She asked me lots of times."

"No she didn't," Cheryl said, a pleading note creeping into her voice.

"Yes, Cheryl, she did. Just because you refused to talk to her about it doesn't mean she didn't try to ask you."

"I loved Holly—" Cheryl began.

"Of course you did. We all loved Holly," Bradley said firmly. "But she knew there was something wrong."

Penelope sat back in her chair and listened to Cheryl Anderson cry and to Joey offering her a new tissue.

"But you showed me her birth certificate listing your names," Joey said, placing the tissue box back on the desk.

"Rachel used my name when she went to the hospital. We used to switch names all of the time in school, swap out of classes to see if the teachers noticed. She didn't have insurance and I did, so I gave her my ID for doctor visits or whatever. We weren't identical but we looked so much alike back then. I was engaged to Brad and Rachel thought...well, I don't know what she thought. I was as surprised as you when I found out she used our names at the hospital."

"And Holly suspected something like that had happened?" Joey said.

"She was always asking why there weren't any pictures of Cheryl pregnant with her. One time she found a picture of us right after our college graduation and Cheryl was obviously not pregnant when she would have been about ready to have Holly. I slipped and told her the year, forgetting that she would be old enough to figure it out. When she was younger we could make excuses, but finding that picture...I think it confirmed some of the things she was thinking," Brad said. "Later she became obsessed with the idea she was adopted or switched at birth. I ran out of things to say to her."

"Did you ever think to tell her the truth?" Joey asked.

"Detective, how do you turn to your child and tell them that you've been lying to them for their whole life? How do you explain that you lied to protect them?" Cheryl asked, anger cutting through her tears.

"I told her," Bradley said in a hoarse whisper.

"What?" Cheryl said quietly.

"I told her the truth. That's why she ran out that night." Bradley's voice broke and his chair scraped the floor as he pushed back from the table.

"Wait a minute, Mr. Anderson," Joey said firmly. "This is the first time you've mentioned anything about this. Tell me exactly what happened."

Bradley sighed loudly and Penelope watched him from the corner of her eye stand up and begin pacing.

"I came home from work and she was in her room, working on the computer. You were out somewhere with the boys. Her notebook was lying on the kitchen counter. It was lying there open, and I saw that she'd written a letter to Randall Madison, asking him to meet her."

Cheryl sighed. "Why didn't you tell me, Brad?"

"I don't know, Cheryl," Bradley said. "But seeing his name there and realizing she found her way to him after all those years, out of millions of people she guessed the truth. I went to her room, asked her about the letter. She panicked, told me it was nothing, tried make it seem like it was a school project. But I knew. I knew she had figured it out. So I told her the truth."

"What exactly did you tell her, Mr. Anderson?" Joey asked, scribbling down notes as they talked.

"I told her that Randall Madison was her father, at least that's what her mother had told us. I also told her that her real mother was her Aunt Rachel, who died when Holly was only a baby."

Cheryl cried in her seat as her husband spoke.

"How did she react?" Joey asked.

"She cried at first. And then she was furious. At all of us. She grabbed her bag and ran out and that was it. Until you called us." His voice broke at the end.

"I told you it was a mistake for her to know," Cheryl said.

"Why was it a mistake, Mrs. Anderson?" Joey asked.

"Because she was happy before she knew. She was a happy little kid. My sister was..." Cheryl paused, searching for words, "...she was reckless. She couldn't take care of Holly and she knew it. We agreed to help her when the baby was born until she could get herself together, get a solid job and a place to live." Cheryl reached for a fresh tissue and continued, her voice getting stronger while recounting the story. "She would disappear for days at a time, sometimes weeks, leaving the baby with us. And then Rachel died. A year later she was gone."

"What happened to her?" Joey asked.

"She overdosed on heroin," Cheryl said quietly. "I didn't want Holly to know about how her mother was, always in trouble somehow. We told her my twin sister, her Aunt Rachel, had died in an accident. And I prayed every day that Holly would never find out the truth."

"We lost her, Cheryl, because we didn't tell her the truth," Bradley said.

Cheryl shifted in her chair, her voice hardening. "No. We lost her because someone took her from us. And you," she said to Joey, "have to promise me you'll find out who killed her."

*   *   *

After the Andersons left, Joey returned to the interrogation room where Penelope waited.

"Did you hear all of that?" Joey asked quietly, closing the door behind him.

"I feel so bad for them," Penelope said.

"I feel bad for Holly," Joey said, sliding the chair out next to Penelope and sitting down.

"She was upset when she heard the truth about her parents not being her real parents, I get that. But what does that have to do with her murder? I don't get the connection."

"Unfortunately, I don't either. I've been over the evidence dozens of times and I'm still not seeing it." Joey sighed and shook his head.

"I guess I should get going," Penelope said, feeling a bit at a loss to help him.

"Wait, I have to talk to you about Nancy," he said, putting his hand on her arm.

Penelope felt a tinge of dread tighten her chest.

"I'm going to take care of that ticket she gave you. Do you have it on you?" Joey asked, glancing at Penelope's bag.

"I have it somewhere. But you don't have to do that," Penelope said.

"It's my fault you got it," Joey said, looking down at the table. "I slipped up and told her that you and I had reconnected and things got complicated, but she knows whatever she thought we had is over now."

"That does sound complicated," Penelope said, deflating a bit. "Joey, you don't have to explain your relationship or pay my ticket. I can take care of it myself. I don't want to get in the middle of things with you and Nancy." Penelope said the woman's name with a touch of distaste.

"There's nothing to get in the middle of. That's the point. She harassed you because she's jealous. She admitted it. So that's my fault, not yours. Hand it over," he said, holding his palm up.

Penelope found the envelope in her bag and handed it to Joey.

"I've told her not to bother you again."

"We'll see," Penelope sniffed, "she seemed pretty determined to send me a threatening message this morning."

"If you see her again and she's not totally professional, let me know. After all this is done," he waved around the interview room, "we'll see where we are with everything. But so you know, she's not my girlfriend. Never was."

Penelope nodded, a bit relieved, but still feeling the need to tread carefully when it came to Joey's personal life. "I have a big day tomorrow. I'm going to head home."

"Can I take you for something to eat, cheer you up?" Joey asked. "I'm going to be off in an hour or so."

"Not tonight. Let's do it another time," Penelope said.

"Go home and get some rest. I'll be in touch. Let me walk you out," he offered.

"That's okay. I can find my own way."

CHAPTER 24

The next day was a blur of work, an extra-long fifteen hours of filming. When Penelope got home that evening she was exhausted, trudging in through the kitchen door and dropping her bag on the base of the coat stand.

"Pen, you're home," Max said.

"Hey, Max. What are you up to?"

"I'm celebrating," he said, nodding to a champagne flute in his hand. He poured a matching glassful, handing it to Penelope.

"What are you celebrating? It would be nice to hear some good news," Penelope said, brightening slightly.

"MTV picked up our pilot. We're signed to thirteen episodes. I got a job, Pen. We start filming next week."

"That's so cool, Max, Congratulations," Penelope said, touching her glass to his. "What did Arlena say? I'm sure she's thrilled for you."

Max finished off his champagne then refilled the glass. "She and Dad are both pretty stoked. And I'll be in the city, so I'll be close by."

"I can't wait to see the show."

"You'll see it. You know you're always welcome to stay with me when you're in the city." Max leaned down to kiss her.

Penelope stood still, exhaustion rooting her to the spot.

Maybe she should let Max kiss her. There was no harm now that things were sort of awkward with Joey. She looked up into his eyes, anticipating his kiss.

Max's expression changed from jovial flirting to serious and Penelope saw a touch of fear in his eyes. He brushed her lips with his once and then leaned down to give her a full kiss. She kissed him back, stepping closer to him and putting an arm around his neck.

"What do we have here?" Randall interrupted loudly from the doorway. Max and Penelope jerked apart, Penelope turning away, her face burning red.

"You ever hear of knocking, Dad?" Max asked, laughing nervously.

"Knocking on what? You guys are in a room without doors."

"Hi, Mr. Madison," Penelope said, wishing she could melt into the floor and disappear.

"Don't mind me. I'm heading out," he said. He clapped his son on the shoulder and grabbed his coat from the hooks by the door. "See you tomorrow," he added as he left.

Max turned back to Penelope and said, "He's gone." He leaned in to kiss her again but Penelope put her hand on his shoulder instead.

"I'm beat, Max. See you tomorrow?"

"Maybe. I have to go to the city for a meeting about the show. But I'll be around after that."

"I'll see you later then. Good night." She placed her champagne glass on the counter and walked around him to head upstairs. Closing her bedroom door, she sat down heavily on her bed, thinking about what had happened. Kissing Max had been nice, but the whole time she couldn't stop thinking about Joey.

She took a shower, standing under the water until it started turning cold, her mind bouncing between Joey and Max, making mental pro-con lists for both of them. By the time she climbed under her covers and switched off her bedside lamp, she'd decided to go in a different direction altogether. She'd focus on her work try to forget about having a relationship with either of them.

CHAPTER 25

Penelope got in early the next morning and began working on ideas for the wrap party menu. She'd had a solid night's sleep and felt renewed, remembering a bit regretfully about her vow the night before to leave her man drama behind and work as hard as she could on her business.

Arlena and Sam ate lunch with everyone in the tent, mingling and laughing with the other cast members and some of the crew. Sal joined their table after everyone had finished eating and called an impromptu table read of the next scene they were filming. Penelope asked Francis to bring them coffee and a tray of fruit and desserts.

"Thanks, Pen, you're a peach," Sal said, waving to her from the table in the center of the room.

Penelope noticed several crew members lingering at their tables, either watching the actors practice their lines or talking quietly amongst themselves. She walked around the tent, straightening tablecloths, tucking abandoned chairs under tables and picking up forgotten plates and trays.

Freddie, one of the production interns, sat at a table in the corner writing in a composition book. He glanced occasionally at his phone or around the room.

"How are you doing, Freddie?" Penelope asked as she approached his table to clear away a few dirty plates.

"Oh, hey," he said. "It's all good today."

"Good. Did you get enough to eat?" Penelope asked, stacking more plates from the adjoining tables.

"Oh, yeah. It was good, thanks," he said, ducking his head and continuing to write in his notebook. He placed his heavily tattooed forearm over the page to obstruct her view, but Penelope could see that it was a screenplay. She noticed a header that read "Int. David's Apartment. Day."

"Working on a script?" Penelope asked casually, still busying herself with cleaning up around him.

He stopped writing and looked up at her. "I'm almost finished the first draft," he said, shrugging his bony shoulders.

"Good for you," Penelope said. "What's it about?" she asked, wiping her hands on her apron.

"Nothing. Well, it's...not *nothing*. It's a sci-fi horror story about a death metal band that makes a pact with the Devil to get famous. They get sucked into an alternate universe and they have to find their way out."

"Wow. That sounds interesting," Penelope said, tucking her hands into her pockets under her apron. "Working on a project with someone like Sal will look good on your resume. I won't be surprised if you get a script produced someday. I can say I knew you when."

Freddie peered shyly up at her. "That's the dream, it's such a competitive business, though. It's hard to break through unless you know somebody."

"Keep doing what you're doing. You're in the right place to get discovered, at least," Penelope said.

"I suppose." Freddie's phone vibrated on the table between them and Penelope saw the contact name BRAWL pop onto the screen with a text message below it that read. "Done. 5K. DIK."

Freddie snatched the phone from the table and clicked the button to darken the screen. He stood up and tucked it in his front jeans pocket, stretching his arms over his head. "Thanks again for lunch. See you around." He grabbed his notebook and jacket and headed towards the other end of the tent.

"Yep. Later. Good luck with your script," Penelope said to his back as he left.

When Penelope got home from work that night she heard Randall's voice coming from the library. She sighed as she stood in the hallway, disappointed that her plan of curling up with a book in front of the fireplace before bed wouldn't happen. She peeked into the room as she passed and saw the back of Randall's head sitting next to a redheaded woman, and Max in one of the flanking chairs with Zazoo perched on his lap.

Max noticed her arrival and waved her into the room. Randall and his guest turned towards her.

"Hi," she said slowly, surprised to see one of the actresses from the movie in her library. Then she remembered Randall meeting the buxom redhead at Sal's dinner party.

"We're going to watch Max's pilot," Randall said, draping his arm around the woman's shoulders as they turned back to the TV.

"Come and watch it with us, Pen," Max said. He scratched Zazoo's ears with one hand and held a remote control in the other.

"Another time. I've got some work to do before bed."

"Goodnight, Pen," Randall said distractedly, focusing his attention back on his guest. She saw a brief moment of disappointment on Max's face but by the time she reached the doorway and looked back he had turned on the TV and his attention was focused on the screen. Penelope paused for a moment in the doorway to watch the opening credits. Seven young people who she did not recognize, except for Max, all with famous last names were sitting in a rooftop hot tub in Manhattan. A montage of scenes flashed across the screen showing the group arguing, dancing at clubs, laughing and drinking. Penelope had a good idea of what the show was going to be like after a few seconds.

CHAPTER 26

Sal and Paige hosted Sunday dinner again that weekend, serving another delicious meal, this time a French-inspired spread with caramelized beef tenderloin and grilled organic pork chops. After dinner Sal once again pulled the actors into the study to go over his plans for the final week.

"Can I go over a few things with you for the wrap party?" Penelope asked Paige as they stood up from the dinner table.

"Sure. Let's go in here," Paige motioned to the kitchen.

Penelope was hoping she'd suggest they stay in the dining room or go to the barn outside so she could avoid another meeting with their chef. "Sure," she said, reluctantly. The two of them pushed through the swinging door and into the kitchen where the chef and Charles were wrapping up leftover food and stacking dishes next to the sink.

The chef glanced up, his face red and sweaty under the bright kitchen lights, and then looked back down at the soup he was ladling into a storage container. Charles nodded at them as they made their way to the island. Paige propped her bony hip against the countertop and gave Penelope her attention, a glass of wine cocked in her other hand.

Penelope opened her notebook and began. "I was thinking we'd do something more upscale for the wrap party," she said, pointing to a menu she had outlined on the page. "Slow roasted prime rib, pesto grilled chicken and then some roasted root vegetables in keeping with the season."

"Very original," the chef muttered under his breath.

Penelope ignored him and looked at Paige, who was reading the page in front of her.

"This is fine, Penelope. I like it. Ignore Jackson. He's a jerk." She raised her glass in a toast towards her chef.

The chef ignored her and poured the rest of the soup in the container, slapping the lid on top of it. "Finish this up, will you, Charles? I've got to go home and pack."

"Sure, Chef," Charles said.

Jackson walked past Paige and Penelope, grabbed his jacket from the hook by the door and left without another word.

"Jackson is very temperamental," Paige chuckled. "But Sal loves him. He's heading to Tuscany tomorrow, and we'll meet him at the house there next week. I guess it's takeout until we leave, right Charles? Poor Charles always gets the worst of him."

"It's fine. I've been cleaning all night so we're in good shape," he said. He walked over to the island and glanced down at the menu. "I think this will be very nice. We can use the rust colored tablecloths and white candles. Fall colors to tie in the name of the movie."

"I love that idea," Penelope said. "What do you think about running a red carpet from the house to the barn as a way to direct the guests?"

"Perfect," Paige said, nodding. "Charles can ask about renting one."

Arlena came through the swinging door. "We're done, Pen. Ready?"

"I think we're set here. Unless you have any questions, Paige?"

"I think we're doing fine. I knew I could leave everything to you," Paige said, finishing her glass of wine.

CHAPTER 27

Penelope sat in the cab of the truck the next afternoon, checking off her to-do list. She had to order all of the food for the last week of filming as well as for the wrap party on Sunday, tally up her team's hours and get them to production for payroll, and submit three bids on upcoming jobs.

She hoped she and her team could go right into another film with maybe a week off in between. Two of the bids were for local jobs in New York and one was in California. Penelope always liked to work closer to home, but thought a change of scenery would do her some good. Either way, they would go wherever they won the bid.

Penelope's phone buzzed on the dashboard and she glanced at it. AMT SECURITY flashed on the screen. She snatched up the phone and swiped open the screen to answer.

"Hello?"

"Hello, this is AMT Security Systems calling. Is this Penelope Sutherland?"

"This is Penelope," she said, her chest tightening.

"Can you confirm your security word?"

"Zazoo," Penelope said quickly.

"Thank you. I'm calling to report an alarm at your

residence, a possible front door push in. Are you currently at home?" The woman's voice sounded tinny and far away.

"No, I'm at work. But someone should be home. There's been a break in at our house?"

"That's what the system is reporting. It's possible someone entered and didn't disarm the system. This is the contact number we have."

"This is my cell phone," Penelope said.

"Is there a number we can call at the residence?" the woman asked. Penelope could hear her typing on a keyboard in the background.

"No. We don't have a landline, and I don't have anyone's phone number who might be there. My housemate does though," Penelope said. "Arlena Madison, you should have her info too."

"We've attempted to call her, but only get a voicemail. We've called the police and they are en route to your residence now," the woman said.

"What should I do now?" Penelope stammered, looking around the cab of the truck.

"We advise caution, ma'am," the woman said. "Please do not attempt to enter your residence until it has been confirmed by the police to be safe. We've opened an incident ticket and will follow up with you after we get confirmation from the unit they've dispatched."

"Thank you," Penelope said.

The line clicked and went silent. Penelope pulled the phone away from her ear and stared at it for a moment before sliding it into her bag.

Pulling the bag over her shoulder, she jumped down from the truck and walked to the prep tent where her chefs were getting the dinner salads ready.

"Francis," she said. All four of her team glanced up at her.

"The alarm is going off at my house. I don't know what's happening yet."

"We've got everything covered here, Boss. Go do what you have to," he said, a concerned look on his face.

She thanked them and walked towards the trailers. She knew they were filming interior scenes in the warehouse today which was on the edge of the lot right past them.

Penelope saw Kelley emerging from the warehouse, her makeup bag slung heavily over her shoulder. "Kelley, are they still filming?"

"I think they're wrapping soon, though," she said. Her hair was bright pink today and Penelope thought maybe it was a wig this time. She looked like one of the Pink Ladies in *Grease*.

"There may have been a break-in at our house. I'm waiting for our security company to call back."

"Oh no. You guys are having a rough time lately."

"It sure seems that way. Hey, I haven't seen your assistant around lately."

"Sal said I had to let her go," Kelley said, looking down at her shoes. "The thing with the lip gloss."

"Oh, I'm sorry," Penelope said.

"I'm lucky he didn't fire me, too. She admitted that she left the trailer unlocked. I had to go through all of the other makeup and lotions and toss a bunch of stuff to be sure nothing else had been tampered with."

"Do you think your assistant did the tampering?"

"Not sure. I can't imagine she'd do something like that. I've known her since cosmetology school, worked with her a lot," Kelley said, lost in thought for a moment. "I have to get back in there. I'm running out to grab more mascara. It's a crying scene today."

"Listen, the next time they break will you tell Arlena I'm heading home to see what's—"

Penelope's phone rang and she snatched it out of her back pocket. AMT SECURITY. She waved her phone at Kelley and answered it, quickly putting the phone up to her ear. Kelley nodded, whispered that she would give Arlena the message and walked towards her trailer.

"Is this Penelope Sutherland?" the woman's voice asked.

"This is Penelope."

"Can you confirm your security word, please?"

"Zazoo," Penelope said, sighing. "What is going on at the house?"

"Thank you, ma'am. We have received notification from the police that your front door was breached as our alarm system reported."

Penelope's heart sank. She began walking towards the parking lot. "The police are there now?"

"Yes, ma'am. Reporting an injured party at the residence," the woman said in an even voice, betraying no emotion.

"Injured? Who was injured?" Penelope asked, breaking into a jog.

"Police are reporting an injured party at the residence, but we have no further information." The woman's voice remained calm, which Penelope took some comfort from.

"I'm on my way," Penelope said. She hung up and unlocked her truck. She sped through town and onto the parkway, keeping on the lookout for police cars. One in particular.

CHAPTER 28

When Penelope turned onto her street she saw three police cars and an ambulance in her driveway. Randall sat on the back bumper of the ambulance holding a cold pack against his head, an EMT studying his face.

Penelope emerged from her car and hurried up the driveway. "Mr. Madison, are you okay?"

Randall looked up. "Hey, Pen. Yeah, yeah, don't worry about it. I'm fine. Just a bump," he said, pointing to the crown of his head. The EMT dabbed a wad of gauze that had antiseptic on it to a cut on his eyebrow.

An officer stood on the wide brick porch at the front door, his hands resting on his thick utility belt. He noticed Penelope approaching the house and spoke into the radio clipped to his shoulder.

"What happened?" Penelope asked Randall, getting a closer look at his injuries. His right eye was swollen and his eyebrow cut, the blood already dark and clotted. A bruise darkened his left cheek. "You look terrible."

"Thanks, Pen," Randall said, chuckling. He pulled a cigarette pack out of his jacket pocket but put it back after the EMT shook her head no. "Stupid jerk jumped me from behind. I was asleep upstairs, I was out late last night, and I hear your little dog barking his ass off and the damn alarm blaring. I come downstairs, the front door's closed and I'm half asleep, I head to the kitchen to turn the damn thing off. Next thing I know I'm face down in the hallway."

"The front door was closed? They said on the phone that's where the break-in was," Penelope said, glancing at the officer in front of her house.

"I don't know, Pen. He must have closed the door behind him," Randall said, wincing as the EMT applied a gooey ointment to his eyebrow.

"I'm going to go see what's going on," Penelope said. "I'll be back." She walked farther up the driveway and climbed the porch steps. "Hi, I'm Penelope Sutherland. I live here."

The uniformed officer held out his hand to stop her from entering the house. "Can't let you in right now, ma'am. This is an active scene."

Penelope glanced under his arm and into the front hallway. One of the policemen was crouched down, examining the hallway carpet. Penelope guessed that's where they'd found Randall. She heard heavy footsteps on the stairs and looked up to see Officer Jenkins descending, a frown on her tanned face.

"Perfect," Penelope muttered, taking a step back from the door. She wasn't particularly interested in another run-in with Officer Jenkins.

"Who's in charge here?" Penelope asked the officer, who gazed out over the yard at the golf course across the street.

"Officer Nancy Jenkins is senior officer on the scene," he said, glancing down at her.

Penelope thanked him, barely containing the urge to grind her teeth. She turned and headed back down the porch steps towards the ambulance. A dark sedan pulled up behind her Range Rover and Joey stepped out, quickly slamming the door and hurrying up the lawn towards her.

"Penny, you all right?" he asked. He squeezed her upper arm tightly when he reached the ambulance.

"I'm fine. I wasn't here when it happened. Randall on the other hand..." She glanced at Randall, who had his head tilted towards the EMT as she placed a bandage over his eyebrow.

"Mr. Madison, did you get a look at your attacker?" Joey asked.

"No, he was wearing a ski mask, I think. But I saw something...a tattoo on his arm. He was wearing gloves but I saw a skull on his wrist right above it. Then he hit me again here," Randall pointed to his eyebrow, "and I blacked out for a minute."

Joey scratched notes in his leather flip pad. "Can you maybe sketch for me what you saw?" He handed Randall the pad and pen. "It would be good to get it from you now while you still have a fresh memory of it."

"I'm no artist, but I'll try," Randall said, studying the blank piece of paper. The EMT finished with him and went inside her ambulance to retrieve more supplies.

"Detective," Officer Jenkins waved him over from the front porch. "A word?"

Joey's jaw twitched and he said, "Excuse me a moment, will ya?"

She watched Joey make his way onto the porch and over to Officer Jenkins. Officer Jenkins stood easily, her hands tucked on her utility belt, a faint smile on her lips. Joey had his back to Penelope but she saw his broad shoulders were tense through his suit jacket. He pointed at the house as he spoke to Officer Jenkins, then folded his arms over his chest.

Penelope couldn't make out what they were saying, but she saw Officer Jenkins expression evolve from slightly happy, to vaguely concerned, to tightly angry in a matter of moments. Joey turned around and glanced at Penelope and Randall and then turned back to her motioning to them as he made another point.

Officer Jenkins uncrossed her arms and straightened her jacket, stepping around Joey without saying a word. She called back over her shoulder to the officer guarding the door and together they walked down the steps away from the porch. As they passed Penelope and Randall at the back of the ambulance she said, "Your hero is in charge now. Have a nice day."

The two of them got in one of the parked patrol cars and backed out of the driveway, Officer Jenkins staring at the house and Joey from the passenger seat.

"Penny, can you come up here please?" Joey called down to her from the porch.

She walked back up the steps and joined him. "What was that all about?" she asked, motioning in the direction of the driveway.

Joey sighed, unable to hide his frustration. "It's...here's the thing," he said. "I didn't report her for what she pulled the other morning...that thing with you. That stupid ticket." Joey shifted his weight and put his hands in his pockets under his opened suit jacket. "I just paid it. But I pulled her aside and told her to keep her distance. Next thing I know, she's at your house." He shook his head in disbelief.

Penelope had no idea how to respond. Instead she asked, "Can I get inside? See what kind of damage there is?"

"Yes," Joey said. "Come on, let's take a look." He ushered her in the front door. Joey called one of the uniformed officers over and asked him to bring him up to speed.

"We have point of entry here," the young officer said, pointing to the front door. "The door isn't damaged. It was either unlocked or the intruder had a key. Then the victim was attacked here." He took a few steps into the hallway and indicated a place on the floor. "We haven't determined if anything is missing and we see no other damage to the home. Maybe Miss..."

"Sutherland," Joey said quickly.

"Sutherland could take a look around and inform us of any missing property," he finished.

"Sure. Let's go," Joey said, motioning to the stairs.

Penelope and Joey made their way through all of the rooms upstairs. Penelope didn't notice anything out of the ordinary. Her jewelry box, which held a few sentimental pieces, was undisturbed and Penelope guessed that maybe the intruder hadn't come upstairs at all. Heading back downstairs, they checked the dining room and the library and then Arlena's suite of rooms, finding nothing missing or damaged in there either. Arlena did have a small safe in her closet for her more expensive jewelry, but the closet was undisturbed and the safe intact.

Penelope turned to follow Joey out of Arlena's bedroom, but at the last minute she froze in the doorway, looking back over her shoulder at the empty dog bed in the corner of the room.

"Oh crap," Penelope said.

"What?" Joey asked.

"Zazoo. He's gone."

Randall stood up from the back of the ambulance and watched the EMT close the doors. She handed him a packet of gauze and ointment and encouraged him to follow up with his doctor about the bump on his head.

"Trust me, this hard head has been knocked around worse than this," he said, pointing to his head and winking at her.

The EMT shook her head at him and departed, backing the ambulance back down the steep driveway.

Penelope called to him from the porch. "Where is Zazoo?"

"What? I don't know." Randall walked towards the house and joined them up on the porch, bouncing Joey's notepad off of his thigh. "He was here before. It was his barking that woke me up in the first place."

"He's not here," Penelope said. "He probably ran out in all of the commotion. The front door was wide open when I got here. Usually the electric fence keeps him in the yard but if he's really scared, he'll run through it."

"You heard the dog barking before you heard the alarm?" Joey asked.

"That's how it was," Randall said.

"And you didn't see or hear anything after you were assaulted? Nothing you can tell us about a vehicle or anything else?"

"No. Well, I saw this, like I told you," Randall said, handing Joey's pad back to him.

Joey glanced down at it then tilted it towards Penelope to show her.

Penelope took the pad from him and held it closer, studying the drawing. "I know this," she said quietly. "I know it."

"You recognize this tattoo?" Joey asked.

"Yeah, it's—" Penelope's phone buzzed in her back pocket and she absently pulled it out and glanced at the screen. Seeing Arlena's name there, her heart skipped as she realized Arlena had no idea what was going on at the house or that Zazoo had run off again.

"Arlena, hey. Wait...what? What do you mean? Okay text it to me," Penelope said, hanging up the phone and watching the screen.

"Pen, what is it?" Joey and Randall stared at her, concern on both of their faces.

"It's Arlena. She's very upset...she just got this message," Penelope said turning the phone around for them to read the forwarded text. GOT YOUR DOG, BITCH. SEE HIM ALIVE AGAIN UR CHOICE. QUIT OR HE'S DEAD.

"Let me see that," Joey said, taking her phone and scrolling the message up and down on the screen. "The number has been blocked. Probably a disposable phone."

Randall's face darkened. "Dammit. I can't believe he got over on me. I should have stopped him."

"Wait," Penelope said, grabbing the pad in Joey's hand. "This tattoo. I know who it is. He works with us."

CHAPTER 29

Penelope sped back to the set with Randall in her passenger seat, Joey following her in his car. They pulled into the lot and parked, Penelope jumping from her car and running towards Arlena's trailer, Randall and Joey close behind. When they got there, she knocked on the door and waited impatiently on the steps for the door to open.

Getting no answer, she hurried over to Sam's trailer and knocked on his door. When it opened, Sal was on the other side of the door, an irritated look on his face.

"What is it?" he snapped.

"Is Arlena here?" Penelope asked hurriedly, looking around Sal and into the trailer.

"She's crying in her trailer. I told her to go home. She's a mess, can't work. Something about a dog," Sal said, stepping aside so Penelope could see inside. Sam sat on his couch, looking stunned, his head in his hands. "In fact, this whole thing is shot. I'm calling it off. Production is shutting down. Tell your crew."

Randall stepped up behind Penelope. "Sal, now wait a minute."

"I don't have a minute, Randall. That's the whole point," Sal snapped at him. "This thing has been one disaster after another. I'm done."

"That's crazy, Sal. A few days left and you bail? Come on, that's not the Salvatore I know. What about all the money you've invested? You want to walk away from that?" Randall said.

"I know. It's such a mess," Sal muttered. "What the hell happened to you, Randall?"

"Got jumped by some punk who works for you," Randall said.

"What? Who?" Sal asked.

"Freddie broke into our house and kidnapped our dog, Sal," Penelope said.

"Have you seen your intern today, Mr. Marco?" Joey asked.

"He's right over there," Sal pointed towards the makeup trailer to a retreating figure in an oversized hooded sweatshirt, talking on a cell phone. "I asked him to go find you and let you know we're done. Isn't that why you're here?"

Penelope turned on the stairs and looked where Sal was pointing. Joey took off running with Randall right on his heels. Penelope stood with Sal and watched Joey approach Freddie, grab his arm and spin him around. Then they watched Freddie shove him and take off running. Penelope jumped down from the stairs and ran after them.

Freddie darted towards the catering area and the dining tent, his puffy sweatshirt billowing around his bony frame, his phone still clutched in his hand. Penelope ran as fast as she could towards the tent right behind Joey, passing Randall as he stopped to clutch his stomach, bending over with a cramp. He waved her forward as she slowed to see if he was okay and then sped up again.

Freddie ran around the big tent and towards the end of the lot, heading out into the residential area of South Point. He slowed as he reached a corner, jogging in place but hesitating as speeding cars crossed in front of him. As he prepared to run again, Joey tackled him, knocking him to the ground. His phone skidded across the sidewalk and Penelope snatched it up after she pulled up next to them. She watched Joey pull Freddie's arms behind his back and put handcuffs on his wrists right over the dull green skull tattoo that matched the sketch in Joey's notebook.

Joey pushed Freddie down onto one of the folding chairs in the dining tent, his hands still cuffed behind his back. Several of the cast and crew members gathered close by in an attempt to see what the commotion was about. Joey went through Freddie's pockets, confiscating his wallet and keys.

"Why'd you run, Freddie? Something you want to tell me?" Joey asked as Freddie snarled up at him.

"I don't have to tell you nothin'," Freddie said, his black bangs flopping into his eyes.

Joey flashed a threatening smile. "You better believe you're going to tell me why you broke into Arlena Madison's house earlier today, assaulted her father and stole her dog."

A look of fear nipped at the corners of Freddie's defiant expression.

"That's right. I got you for breaking and entering and assault. Not to mention theft and extortion, and anything else I can think of."

Penelope looked down at the phone in her hand and noticed it was still on an active call. The name BRAWL was on the screen. She raised the phone to her ear and said, "Hello? Who is this?"

There was a click on the other end and the line went dead.

"Who's BRAWL, Freddie?" Penelope asked, showing him the screen of the phone. When he didn't answer and looked away she went back to the phone and scrolled over to his text messages. Finding the one he'd sent to Arlena earlier, she showed him the screen again. "Where is my dog?"

Sal came through the large crowd that had gathered with Arlena, Sam and Randall right behind him. "What the hell is going on now?" he demanded.

"I'm placing Frederick Fitzgerald," Joey said, glancing at the flipped open wallet in his hand, "under arrest for assault, breaking and entering and theft."

"He's the one who has Zazoo?" Arlena said in alarm. "He sent that message? Why would you do that?" she yelled at him angrily, pushing past Sal and standing next to Penelope. Sam stepped forward and placed a hand on her arm, holding her back slightly.

"You stupid bitch. You've got no right to talk to me like that. I did what I had to do," Freddie sneered.

"What are you talking about?" she demanded, her voice straining in anger.

"You don't belong here but you wouldn't quit. All you had to do was quit and I'd get everything I've been working for," he said. "Running over you with a golf cart didn't work and blowing up your face with fish sauce didn't scare you off. Whatever. Sal's shutting down this boring piece of crap anyway, so I win."

"He's not making any sense," Arlena said, looking back at Sal.

Penelope glanced back down at the phone and scrolled over to the recent calls, looking up the last call made. After four rings a woman picked up. "Raw Studios, how can I direct your call?"

Penelope hung up and said to Joey, "Raw Studios in California. Brett Ralston's company. Or as Freddie calls him, BRAWL."

Arlena gasped. "Brett Ralston put you up to all of this? Because I wouldn't act in another one of his stupid movies?"

Freddie's expression crumpled. "He's going to make my movie. He said he'd read my script and give me a job in California if I could get Arlena to quit Sal's movie."

Arlena stared at him in shock while Sam took her hand in his.

"Where is our dog?" Penelope asked, still holding his phone.

"Give it up, kid. Don't make things worse for yourself," Joey advised.

"He's in the trunk of my car," he said under his breath. "The red Camry parked at the edge of the lot."

Murmurs went through the crowd as Joey tossed Freddie's car keys to Penelope. "Go get him. Be careful."

"I'll go with you," Randall said, falling in beside Penelope as she hurried to the lot.

As they approached Freddie's car, Penelope could hear Zazoo's whimpers from the trunk. She hurried to open it, fumbling with the keys at the lock. Randall steadied her hand and they turned the key, popping it open. Zazoo stared up at them from inside a small rusty rabbit cage, surrounded by oily rags, a few tools and some muddy tennis shoes.

"Zazoo!" Penelope said, prying open the cage. He scurried out and happily jumped into her arms, nuzzling her neck with his nose.

"Thank God he isn't hurt," Randall said. "Come on, let's get Arlena out of here."

As they walked back towards the set, they saw Joey leading Freddie towards his police car. He opened the back door and directed Freddie inside, advising him to watch his head on the way in. When he saw Penelope and Randall he waved them over.

"The little guy's okay, huh?" Joey said, scratching the top of Zazoo's head. Zazoo looked at Joey suspiciously but accepted the affection.

"He seems fine. I'm going to get him some water and see what's going on with Arlena," Penelope said. "I'm so glad you were able to help find him. Thanks, Joey."

"It's nothing. I'm glad he's not hurt. I'm taking Freddie to the station, get him booked. I'll give you a call later and fill you in." With one last look at Penelope, Joey slid into his car and sped off.

CHAPTER 30

Arlena and Sam cuddled on the couch in the library that evening, Penelope and Randall sitting in the flanking chairs in front of the fire. Zazoo dozed in the corner of the couch, exhausted from his traumatic day.

"No matter what happens," Randall said, "my baby girl is safe. That's the most important thing."

Arlena sighed. "Safe and out of a job, most likely." She looked up at Sam, who had his arm draped over her shoulders. "But if it weren't for Sal and *Remember the Fall*, I wouldn't have met you, so I suppose it's all been worth it."

"Everything is going to work out fine, babe. Sal's not going to call it off. I bet he just needs some time to cool down."

"I don't know. He was pretty angry," Arlena said. "I'm so embarrassed that it's all because of me, and that all of those people are out of work."

"You didn't do anything wrong," Randall said firmly. "That Ralston idiot—"

The doorbell rang and they all turned their heads towards the doorway. "I'll get it," Penelope said, easing up slowly from her chair.

Joey stood on the front porch, looking tired but also relieved.

"Joey, come in," Penelope said.

"Thanks. I have some information that I wanted to tell you in person. I hope you don't mind me stopping by," he said, stepping into the front hall.

"Not at all." Penelope led him to the kitchen, stopping by the library entrance to tell everyone that Joey was there.

Penelope slid onto one of the kitchen stools and Arlena took the one next to her, folding her hands in her lap.

"I've finished questioning Frederick Fitzgerald and we're investigating his relationship with Brett Ralston," Joey began. "Freddie says Mr. Ralston encouraged him to harass Arlena, and in return he promised to produce a script Freddie was writing. So far Mr. Ralston is denying any arrangement being made, but we found texts and calls between the two of them daily for the past few weeks.

Arlena shook her head and looked at Penelope. "I can't believe that man," she said.

"Freddie admitted to tampering with your makeup, causing your allergic reaction, says Ralston told him exactly what to do. He also sold pictures of you to the tabloids, and he followed you, posing as one of the paparazzi."

Penelope suddenly remembered the group of photographers surrounding their limo and the angry tattooed fist pounding the window.

"And of course there was the golf cart incident, and the break-in here," Joey continued. "He was getting more desperate. He hadn't been able to scare you off and time was running out on your film."

"He admitted to everything?" Penelope asked.

"He's admitted to all of the harassment of Arlena. But he won't admit to having anything to do with Holly Anderson...claims he knows nothing about her death, except for the news reports. We've connected Holly to Brett Ralston, his number shows up in her phone records and she sent him a few emails suggesting she'd be a good stand-in for Arlena, which went unanswered. But since Freddie was taking orders from Ralston, and he's unable to account for his whereabouts on the night she was killed, I think it's safe to say it's only a matter of time before we connect him to her murder. We're running his DNA against what was collected from her body now."

"I can't believe we worked every day with a murderer," Penelope said, shaking her head. "And for a movie?"

"Believe me, I've seen people killed over much less. This Ralston guy was promising Freddie the world. He's a nineteen-year-old kid who thought he saw a ticket to fame. Talking to him, I don't think he imagined it would get as far as it did."

"Thank you, Detective," Arlena said. "I appreciate what you've done for us during all of this." She stood up from her stool and headed back to the library with Sam, who'd joined them in time to catch the last of the conversation.

"Joey, I have to thank you too. This has been a terrible time, but you somehow made it survivable."

"It's nothing. Look, Penny, I want to let you know I'm embarrassed by the mess with Officer Jenkins. I don't want you to think that I somehow—"

"It's nothing," Penelope interrupted. "I should have made sure you were available before I pursued anything—"

"I am available," Joey interrupted.

Penelope looked at him hopefully. "Someone might disagree with you. You know, your tan, possessive friend."

Joey sighed and unbuttoned his jacket, moving around the island and taking the seat next to Penelope. "It's my fault she feels that way." Joey paused for a moment then said, "Here's the thing. I hired her to be my trainer, so we worked out a lot, went for runs together. I asked her to eat with me afterwards a few times. I didn't mean anything by it, just as friends."

Penelope listened to him, welcoming the familiar warm feeling she got whenever he was near.

"It's my fault I didn't make things clear from the beginning. She started getting too familiar, especially at work. I told her a few times to tone it down, but she couldn't spend time with me at the gym without thinking that meant we were dating." Joey looked up at Penelope and then back down at his hands.

"And then I saw you again after all these years and something clicked. I haven't been in too many relationships but I thought with you..." he trailed off. He took Penelope's hand in his and continued, "I invited her over one night to explain it all to her. That I was interested in someone and I couldn't train with her anymore, that she had the wrong idea about us and that I thought it would be better if we didn't have any contact outside of work."

Penelope leaned back against the stool and searched his face.

"I'm sorry she decided to take it out on you, Penny. I didn't tell her how I felt about you or mention your name. I didn't even know how you felt about me before that night." He lowered his voice. "But I wanted to find out."

Penelope leaned in quickly and kissed him on lips. He leaned forward on his stool and kissed her back, shifting around to face her.

When they separated again she said, "I like you too, Joey."

"Pen," Randall called from the library, interrupting the moment.

Penelope sighed quietly. "Yes, Mr. Madison?"

"Champagne! Sal called and the movie is back on. Two more days and you're a wrap. Stubborn old man changed his mind."

"I guess we're not fired," she said to Joey. "Would you like to stay and join us?"

"That's great news, but I can't." Joey stood up and held out his hand, helping her down from her stool. "I have to get back and look into the charges against Mr. Ralston. I've scheduled a call with a detective out in LA."

"In that case I suppose you should get back to work," Penelope said, hiding her disappointment.

"But I'll call you tomorrow, if that's okay," he added quickly.

"Of course," Penelope said, brushing his cheek with her fingertips. "This job will be over by the weekend, and then I'll have some downtime."

"I'll look forward to that," Joey said, bending down to kiss her again.

CHAPTER 31

Penelope pulled up to the Marco's house that Sunday afternoon with her whole team loaded in her Range Rover. She turned around to look at her three chefs in the backseat. "This is the last big day. It's been a rough shoot, so let's put on an amazing party and kiss it goodbye."

Francis grinned from the passenger seat. "It will be good to see the back end of this one."

"You said it," Penelope said. "Let's keep the chatter in the kitchen to a minimum. We're in the boss's house so no gossip about the set or anything that went on before."

They all agreed. Once inside, Penelope set them up in stations in the four corners of the kitchen. Their duties were very similar to the ones on set and Penelope knew her crew would adjust well to the new space.

"Hey guys." Charles pushed his way through the swinging door from the dining room.

"Everyone, this is Charles. He manages the house for the Marcos," Penelope said. The crew waved to him from their stations.

When prompted, Penelope assured Charles that everything was on schedule. She and her crew wore their white starched chef jackets over black and white checkered pants and short white toques. Penelope had asked them to wear their more formal chef gear as opposed to the jeans and t-shirts they wore under their coats on set. They were throwing an elegant party, after all, and she wanted them to look their best.

Penelope glanced out the kitchen door and noticed delivery men carrying long tables in through the barn door. "It's supposed to snow, but not until we'll be getting ready to go."

"I heard about the storm coming," Charles said. "I don't think it's going to be too much where it will cause us any problems." He headed back out to supervise the table delivery.

Paige came through the swinging door then and stopped short when she saw the activity in the kitchen. "Oh, wow, you're here already."

"I hope that's okay," Penelope said.

"Sure. I know we agreed one o'clock. I lost track of time." Paige walked over to the freezer and pulled out a bottle of vodka, pouring some into the empty glass in her hand. She glanced guiltily at Penelope as she took a sip. "These things always set my nerves on edge. But this helps." Paige tilted the glass at Penelope and threw it back, drinking it all in one gulp.

"I know what you mean," Penelope said, turning back to her team. She went over to Francis who was seasoning the roast beef and suggested he place fresh rosemary under the twine he had wrapped around it. "We'll carry over the rosemary and garlic to the roasted potatoes, too." When she looked up again Paige had disappeared out the back door.

The entire cast and crew attended the wrap party. Penelope and her team, along with Charles, helped serve the meal in the barn from a long station in the back of the room. The food had come out smoothly, and Penelope was happy that everyone seemed to be enjoying themselves.

Sal and Paige faced their guests from a long table in the

front of the room. They reminded Penelope of a proud bride and groom. Sam and Arlena sat beside Sal and Randall and the pretty redheaded actress he'd been seeing were at the other end next to Paige. About halfway through dinner, Sal tapped a spoon on his wine glass to get everyone's attention.

The conversation died down and Sal stood up, wine glass in hand.

"I want to thank each and every one of you for your hard work on this project," Sal began. "I have to admit, I didn't know if we were going to make it."

Nervous laughter rippled through the room.

"But somehow we did. This story is a special one to me. I discovered it many years ago and I worked hard to get the screenplay written, right in this building as a matter of fact." Sal pointed at the ceiling and his office above. Paige poured herself another glass of wine as her husband spoke.

"Sometimes the things we love the most take time. But they're worth it in the end. *Salute*," he said, raising his glass.

"*Salute*," the crowd responded from their seats.

Penelope and her crew sat in the kitchen, finally eating their dinner, the party well underway out in the barn.

"Good job, you guys." Penelope forked a piece of roast into her mouth.

"Thanks, Boss," Francis said. "Do you know what's up next for us?"

"I meant to tell you guys. We got two responses out of the three bids. One's a job in Manhattan, three months long that starts two weeks from now. And the other is in California. That one starts in a little over a week and it's a nine-week job." She looked at each of them, waiting for a response. "What do you guys think? The money is about the same. Getting the trucks out to California would mean we'd have to drive out a few days early."

"Springtime in New York?" Francis shrugged. "Sounds good to me."

The others nodded.

"I was thinking that too. When I get back tonight I'll send our acceptance," Penelope said, loving that she had the whole spring locked up with a job close to home. And Joey.

Penelope glanced out of the kitchen window and noticed the snow had started falling, thick and wet. Someone was moving slowly towards the house, slipping here and there on the path leading to the barn. She stood up and opened the door when she realized it was Paige coming up the walk. Penelope stepped out to help her up the steps, which were now slick with snow.

Paige looked up, surprised to see Penelope right next to her. "Penelope," she slurred. "Everything was wonderful."

Penelope guided her into the kitchen, brushing a few flakes from her shoulder. Paige immediately went to the corner cabinet and pulled out a bottle of wine. "Gimme a glass, will you?"

"We just brewed some fresh coffee, Paige," Penelope said, cutting her eyes at Francis. "Would you like some?"

Paige cackled heartily. "Maybe later. Right now I'll take that wine glass I asked for." She put her hand on the counter by the door to steady herself.

Francis glanced quickly at Penelope who shrugged behind Paige's back. He took a glass from the other side of the kitchen and walked it over to her.

"Thanks," she said sleepily, filling it and leaning against the counter to drink.

Penelope's phone buzzed in her coat pocket and she winced. She didn't want Paige to see her talking on the phone, especially if it was a personal call. "Excuse me," she said and stepped into the dining room. Pulling her phone out, grinning to herself when she saw Joey's name.

"Hey." She spoke quietly, glancing through the window in the door at her staff in the kitchen. She could see Paige talking with them as they finished eating dinner.

"I'm good. Glad to hear your voice," Joey said. "You still working?"

"We're coming to the end. Just have to serve coffee and dessert and then clean up," Penelope said. "Then I'm off for two weeks until my next job starts."

"Next job? You know what you're doing already?" Joey asked.

"We've decided we're going to take a job in the city, so I'll be close by."

Joey sighed in relief. "That's awesome news. I was afraid you'd be leaving for some far off location right when we were getting to know each other again."

"No, I'll be here for the next few months at least. I'm looking forward to spending some of that time with you."

"Me too. And I'm looking forward to wrapping up this case."

"So how's it going? Any news with Holly and the DNA?"

"That's one of the reasons I called. I'm going to have to get an elimination sample from you."

"From me? Why?" Penelope asked, alarm pricking her stomach.

"Don't worry. It's just that the only DNA we found on her was from a female. You had contact with the body when you found her. If it's yours, we know that we've got to start looking for another way to prove our case against Freddie."

Penelope sighed. "Should I come by tomorrow?"

"Tomorrow works. Sorry, Penny, but this will really help. I'll get to see you, so that's something."

"No offense, but I can think of much better places to meet than the police station."

Penelope looked back through the window. Paige was pouring more wine. Penelope couldn't imagine how she was going to feel tomorrow.

Joey chuckled. "That's true. I'll make it up to you. How about dinner tomorrow night?"

"That sounds wonderful," Penelope said. "I'll see you tomorrow. I should get back in the kitchen."

"See you tomorrow, Penny Blue."

When she got back in the kitchen, Penelope saw that Charles had come through the back door with a wobbling stack of dinner plates, his hair and jacket covered in snow.

"Oh Charles, you're soaked," Paige shrieked loudly, surprising everyone around her. "Just think, two days from now we'll be in a place where it never snows."

Charles gave Paige a polite nod and continued to the sink. Francis jumped up from his seat to help him stack the dishes on the counter.

"I hate the damn snow," Paige slurred from the corner, her voice lowering again. "I can't believe we have to live in a cold snowy state like New Jersey. It's so glamorous and romantic. And at my in-law's tiny house on top of it." Paige spoke to no one in particular as Penelope and her crew busied themselves around her, clearing down their stations and cleaning the kitchen.

"If we're really lucky we'll get a blackout like we did last time. How's that for modern life? The minute it starts snowing the lights go out," Paige said bitterly, sipping her wine.

Charles walked quickly over to Paige and took her wrist in his hand, his expression concerned. "Mrs. Marco, maybe you should go lay down for a while. It's been a long day."

"When did the lights go out?" Francis asked.

"The last time it snowed," she said, glaring at Charles. She struggled to pull her hand from him but he held it tighter.

"I live in town and we were fine up there," Francis said, stretching cling wrap over bowls filled with salad greens.

"I think you should go lay down," Charles said again, attempting to take Paige's wine glass from her. Penelope turned and watched them from the counter, surprised at Charles' forcefulness towards Paige. Up until now she'd only seen his good natured side, and thought of him as someone who would never challenge his employer.

Penelope's spine straightened and a wave of cold nausea rolled through her stomach. "Sal said the power stayed on up here. We lost ours for a few hours out in Glendale..." Penelope trailed off when she saw the look of panic on Paige's face.

Paige threw her wine glass at the wall and pushed Charles aside, lunging for the knife block that sat on the counter next to her. She pulled one of the long chef knives from the block and waved it drunkenly near his face, causing him to back up from her. She spun and waved it in a wide arc at the rest of the room. Everyone froze, shock rooting them to the spot.

"Paige, what are you doing?" Penelope asked cautiously.

"You knew it was me," she said, waving the knife at Francis. He looked at Penelope with an expression of confused fear.

"Knew it was you? What do you mean?" Penelope asked gently. Charles eased away from her along the wall toward the back door.

"Ask him, he knows," Paige said, waving the knife again at Charles.

Penelope looked at Charles but he was watching Paige. The knife appeared to be too heavy for her wrist, which wilted the longer she tried to hold it up. The back door swooshed open and Sal entered, followed by Arlena.

"I've been saving this bottle for a night like—what the hell?"

Sal stopped when he saw Paige waving the knife around. Arlena locked eyes with Penelope behind the kitchen island and Penelope silently urged her to stay calm.

"You. It was you too," Paige slurred.

"What? What the hell has gotten into you? Give me that." Sal moved toward Paige and attempted to take the knife from her, but she backed up and swung it wildly at him, slicing his hand, which started bleeding onto the floor.

"Paige!" he yelled, staring at his bleeding hand in disbelief.

Penelope reached into her chef coat pocket and discretely pulled out her phone. Hiding it below the countertop, she swiped it open and texted Joey the message PAIGE MARCO 911.

Paige started shouting, but her words ran together and it was unclear what she was saying. Penelope saw her crew shifting around uncomfortably, unsure of what to do.

Sal approached Paige again, holding his bleeding hand out to her. "Paige, listen, give me the knife. Let's talk about this."

"Talk about what? About your pet project that *you* discovered? That *she* is starring in?" Paige waved the knife at Arlena with renewed vigor. "You know I gave you that book, that I loved it. That it would have been a perfect project for me. But you kept me out of it, waited too long so I'd be too old. I know how you think."

Sal raised his voice. "I told you a million times. I don't want my wife in my movies. I won't allow my wife in a movie where she's going to be in bed with another man. How many times do I have to tell you that?"

"The worst mistake I ever made was marrying you," Paige spat at him. "You were supposed to make my career but you ended it. And no kids...no kids because I wanted to act. Actresses make terrible mothers, that's what you said." Her shoulders shrank and Sal moved away from her, looking around the room at everyone's stunned faces.

"Paige." Penelope eased towards her. "What happened the night the lights went out?"

Paige sighed and propped her elbow on the counter, still holding the knife in her limp hand.

"All I wanted to do was ask her," she nodded at Arlena, "to not do my movie. This was *my* movie. So I went to your house to ask you nicely to go away." She looked at Arlena and tears began to slide down her cheeks.

"I had a few drinks to get my nerve up and drove over to your house in all of that snow. It was so dark I couldn't see anything. But I saw you, outside of your house, out in the driveway."

"That wasn't me," Arlena said quietly. "That was my sister, Holly Anderson."

"No, it was you," Paige said, laughing. "Don't tell me it wasn't you. Remember, I turned you around and asked you to please, please go away and tell Sal you changed your mind about the whole thing? I told you...tell Sal you had found something else. I needed you to understand."

Penelope moved closer to Paige, who seemed to be losing her grip on reality as the story went on.

"But you screamed at me. Told me I was crazy, called me a crazy drunk. So I hit you," Paige said.

Sal shook his head. "Paige, what have you done?"

"Then you fell and hit your head on the driveway," Paige continued. "I dragged you back to the car. I knew I shouldn't have hit you. I was going to drop you off at the hospital, but you weren't breathing. I panicked and pushed you out onto the side of the road. And I drove home."

"She was just a kid," Arlena said. "A girl who never did anything to you, you crazy bitch."

Paige scoffed at Arlena, and for a moment seemed to forget she was holding the knife. Penelope took a chance and moved two steps closer to her while she was distracted. Francis inched up behind Penelope subtly, realizing that sudden movements wouldn't be the best idea around the unstable woman.

Out of the corner of her eye, Penelope saw flashing lights approaching through the kitchen window.

"I can't believe you would do this to me, you useless..." Sal began.

Penelope gave him a harsh stare, willing him to be quiet. She took another step closer to Paige.

Paige suddenly realized how close Penelope had gotten and her body became rigid. She sprang and waved the knife wildly at Penelope, bringing it down through the air in a large arcing motion towards her head. Arlena screamed and Penelope ducked away at the last minute, feeling the knife's blade graze across her shoulder. Paige swayed drunkenly on her feet and Penelope saw her chance, lunging towards her and pushing her against the counter. She grabbed Paige's wrist and squeezed as tight as she could until she heard the knife clatter onto tiles between their feet. Sal rushed up from the other side and grabbed Paige in a bear hug, pinning her arms to her sides, the blood from his hand running down Paige's sweater.

The back door opened and a police officer stepped inside, his gun drawn and aimed at the three of them. "Everybody freeze," he directed.

"Look, Sal, the police," Paige said drunkenly. "What are they doing here?"

Joey spoke through the car window to the officer, instructing him to take Paige Marco into custody. After the car drove away with Paige secured in the backseat, Joey walked through the snowy backyard past all of the lingering partygoers towards Penelope. She stood on the back steps of the kitchen, her arms wrapped around herself against the cold, the shoulder of her chef coat and her t-shirt underneath sliced open. He climbed the steps and looked through the hole catching a glimpse of the thin cut across her shoulder, now held together by three butterfly bandages. He pulled her into a gentle hug, breathing warmly on her neck.

"Penny, thank God you weren't hurt," he said gruffly.

"I'm fine. I'm glad you got my text." She smiled up at him. "And figured out what I meant."

"Me too," Joey said, releasing her but keeping his hands on her upper arms. "We're going to have to get statements from you and your guys. Should be pretty easy to bring charges against Paige for Holly's murder since she confessed to it in front of half a dozen people."

"We'll do whatever you need," Penelope said. "Everyone is still waiting inside. Sal's going to have to get stitches, I think, but he's refusing to go to the hospital until he talks with you."

"How is everyone else doing?" Joey asked.

"I think everyone is in shock. I'm just glad Paige didn't hurt anyone else," she said, glancing down at her shoulder. "Randall and Arlena are devastated. They can't believe Holly turned out to be family and they never got a chance to know her."

"This all seems pretty senseless," Joey said.

Penelope looked up at him and her eyes became glossed over with tears. Suddenly her legs didn't feel like they would hold her up anymore. She leaned into Joey's chest as tears slipped down her cheeks. She watched one of the uniformed officers begin to clear the yard of party guests and a few curious neighbors who had gathered on the sidewalk to get a better look at what was happening.

"Hey, how are you doing?" Joey asked, rubbing her back.

Penny thought for a moment. "It's so sad that Holly had to die for something that seems so pointless. Nothing about her death makes any sense."

Joey pulled her close. "I know. These things never do."

Penelope nodded in his arms, but wasn't ready to look up at him yet.

"Let's get inside. It's freezing out here," Joey said softly.

Penelope took a shaky breath and sighed, pulling away from him and finally feeling strong enough to look into his eyes. "I'm ready."

SHAWN REILLY SIMMONS

Shawn Reilly Simmons was born in Indiana, grew up in Florida, and began her professional career in New York City as a sales executive after graduating from the University of Maryland with a BA in English. Since then Shawn has worked as a bookstore manager, fiction editor, convention organizer, wine consultant and caterer. She has been on the Board of Directors of Malice Domestic since 2003, and is a founding member of The Dames of Detection. Cooking behind the scenes on movie sets perfectly combined two of her great loves, movies and food, and provides the inspiration for her series.

The Red Carpet Catering Mystery Series
By Shawn Reilly Simmons

MURDER ON A SILVER PLATTER (#1)
MURDER ON THE HALF SHELL (#2)
MURDER ON A DESIGNER DIET (#3)
(June 2016)

Available at booksellers nationwide and online

Visit www.henerypress.com for details

Henery Press Mystery Books

And finally, before you go...
Here are a few other mysteries
you might enjoy:

DINERS, DIVES & DEAD ENDS

Terri L. Austin

A Rose Strickland Mystery (#1)

As a struggling waitress and part-time college student, Rose Strickland's life is stalled in the slow lane. But when her close friend, Axton, disappears, Rose suddenly finds herself serving up more than hot coffee and flapjacks. Now she's hashing it out with sexy bad guys and scrambling to find clues in a race to save Axton before his time runs out.

With her anime-loving bestie, her septuagenarian boss, and a pair of IT wise men along for the ride, Rose discovers political corruption, illegal gambling, and shady corporations. She's gone from zero to sixty and quickly learns when you're speeding down the fast lane, it's easy to crash and burn.

Available at booksellers nationwide and online

Visit www.henerypress.com for details

PORTRAIT OF A DEAD GUY

Larissa Reinhart

A Cherry Tucker Mystery (#1)

In Halo, Georgia, folks know Cherry Tucker as big in mouth, small in stature, and able to sketch a portrait faster than buck-shot rips from a ten gauge -- but commissions are scarce. So when the well-heeled Branson family wants to memorialize their murdered son in a coffin portrait, Cherry scrambles to win their patronage from her small town rival.

As the clock ticks toward the deadline, Cherry faces more trouble than just a controversial subject. Between ex-boyfriends, her flaky family, an illegal gambling ring, and outwitting a killer on a spree, Cherry finds herself painted into a corner she'll be lucky to survive.

Available at booksellers nationwide and online

Visit www.henerypress.com for details

A MUDDIED MURDER

Wendy Tyson

A Greenhouse Mystery (#1)

When Megan Sawyer gives up her big-city law career to care for her grandmother and run the family's organic farm and café, she expects to find peace and tranquility in her scenic hometown of Winsome, Pennsylvania. Instead, her goat goes missing, rain muddies her fields, the town denies her business permits, and her family's Colonial-era farm sucks up the remains of her savings.

Just when she thinks she's reached the bottom of the rain barrel, Megan and the town's hunky veterinarian discover the local zoning commissioner's battered body in her barn. Now Megan is thrust into the middle of a murder investigation—and she's the chief suspect. Can Megan dig through small-town secrets, local politics, and old grievances in time to find a killer before that killer strikes again?

Available at booksellers nationwide and online

Visit www.henerypress.com for details

Made in the USA
Lexington, KY
18 September 2017